KU-639-916

For Madison and Riley Cabot

RULES FOR GIRLS

MOVING DAY

Meg Cabot is the author of the phenomenally successful The Princess Diaries series. With vast numbers of copies sold around the world, the books have topped the US and UK bestseller lists for weeks and won several awards. Two movies based on the series have been massively popular throughout the world.

Meg is also the author of the bestselling Airhead trilogy, *All American Girl, All American Girl: Ready or Not, How to Be Popular, Jinx, Teen Idol, Avalon High, Tommy Sullivan Is a Freak*, The Mediator series and the Allie Finkle series as well as many other books for teenagers and adults. She and her husband divide their time between New York and Florida.

Visit Meg Cabot's website at
www.megcabot.co.uk

Also available in audio

ALLIE FINKLE'S
RULES
FOR
GIRLS

MOVING DAY

MEG CABOT

MACMILLAN CHILDREN'S BOOKS

First published 2008 by Macmillan Children's Books

This edition published 2010 by Macmillan Children's Books
a division of Macmillan Publishers Limited
20 New Wharf Road, London N1 9RR
Basingstoke and Oxford
Associated companies throughout the world
www.panmacmillan.com

ISBN 978-0-330-45375-2

Copyright © Meg Cabot LLC 2008

The right of Meg Cabot to be identified as the
author of this work has been asserted by her in accordance
with the Copyright, Designs and Patents Act 1988.

All rights reserved. No part of this publication may be
reproduced, stored in or introduced into a retrieval system, or
transmitted, in any form or by any means (electronic, mechanical,
photocopying, recording or otherwise), without the prior written
permission of the publisher. Any person who does any unauthorized
act in relation to this publication may be liable to criminal
prosecution and civil claims for damages.

7 9 8

A CIP catalogue record for this book is available from
the British Library.

Typeset by Intype Libra Ltd
Printed and bound by CPI Group (UK) Ltd, Croydon, CR0 4YY

This book is sold subject to the condition that it shall not,
by way of trade or otherwise, be lent, resold, hired out,
or otherwise circulated without the publisher's prior consent
in any form of binding or cover other than that in which
it is published and without a similar condition including this
condition being imposed on the subsequent purchaser.

Many thanks to Beth Ader, Jennifer Brown,
Michele Jaffe, Laura Langlie, Abigail McAden
and especially Benjamin Egnatz

Rule #1

Don't Stick a Spatula Down
Your Best Friend's Throat

I like rules. The reason why is, rules help make our lives easier. For instance, the rule about not killing people. Obviously this is a good rule.

Another good rule is *Everything that goes up must come down*. This includes helium balloons. People don't know this, but you shouldn't let helium balloons loose outside, like at weddings or the Olympics or whatever, because what happens is eventually all the helium comes out and the balloons fall down, possibly in the ocean, and sea turtles eat them.

Then they choke to death.

So really that is two rules: *Everything that goes up must come down* and *Don't let go of helium balloons outside*.

Science has a lot of rules (like the one about

1

gravity). So does math (like that five minus three will always be two. That is a rule).

That's why I like science and math. You know where you stand with them, rulewise.

What I'm not so crazy about is everything else. Because there are no rules for everything else.

There are no rules, for instance, for friendship. I mean, besides the one about *Treat your friends the way you'd want them to treat you*, which I've already broken about a million times. Like earlier today when my best friend, Mary Kay Shiner, and I were making the strawberry frosting for her birthday cupcakes.

First of all, who puts *strawberry* frosting on cupcakes? Especially when Mary Kay knows perfectly well one of my rules is *Never eat anything red*.

Although in this case the frosting was pinkish, so technically it was OK. But still.

Mary Kay's babysitter – who is also her family's housekeeper – Carol, was helping us, and Mary Kay wouldn't stop crying, on account of Carol letting me lick the spatula. Like Mary Kay didn't just get to lick the beaters, since it was her birthday. Did anyone hear me complain that all I got was the lousy spatula, even though truthfully I did most of the work, opening the box and all of that? No.

Moving Day

Also, at nine years old you shouldn't cry over things like not getting to lick a spatula.

Sometimes I don't even know why I am friends with Mary Kay. Except that she is the only girl my age who lives on my side of High Street, which I'm not allowed to cross without an adult present since that kid got hit by a car while he was riding his skateboard there.

Which reminds me. Here is another rule: *Always wear a helmet when you're skateboarding, because if a car hits you your brain will splat open and kids like me will spend their time waiting for the cars to go by so they can cross the street looking for bits of your brain the ambulance might have left behind in the bushes.*

Anyway, while I was licking the spatula, Mary Kay was all, 'She's getting more than me!' and 'I want a taste!'

I don't know what I was thinking. I was just so sick of Mary Kay's whining. I mean, half the time I don't think Mary Kay knows how lucky she is, having a babysitter who is also a housekeeper who makes cupcakes for her to take to school on her birthday. We don't have a babysitter who is also a housekeeper, so no one in my family has time to make cupcakes since both my parents work.

So for my birthday I had to bring store-bought

cupcakes from Kroger, and Scott Stamphley said he could taste the chemicals in them.

Plus Mary Kay has parents who will buy her whatever she wants, like a hamster in its own Habitrail, because she is an only child and her parents can Afford It.

Maybe that is what I was thinking about when I said, 'Here, Mary Kay,' and held out the spatula. Maybe I was thinking about how Mary Kay has her very own pet, a hamster (Sparky) with a Habitrail, whereas I only have a dog – Marvin – who I have to share with my whole family.

Maybe that is what I was thinking about when Mary Kay put the spatula into her mouth and I was still holding on to the end.

Maybe that is what I was thinking about when I kind of shoved the spatula into her mouth a little.

I meant it as a joke. A birthday joke.

And OK, I know it was mean. But I just wanted to teach her a lesson about not being so greedy. I meant it in a joking way.

But I should have known Mary Kay wouldn't take it that way. As a joke, I mean.

And I should have known she'd start crying, this time for real, because the spatula went down her throat.

Moving Day

But just a little! Like, it BARELY went down. Maybe it touched her tonsils. But that's it.

Still. This is not a good example of treating your friends as you would want them to treat you. Also, it was all my fault.

I said I was sorry about a million times. But Mary Kay still wouldn't stop crying. Finally I had no choice but to go home and sit in the wheelbarrow in the garage and tell myself it was all my fault; I'd broken the only rule of friendship that there is (which I didn't make up myself).

Although a part of me couldn't help thinking that Mary Kay had broken an important rule, my own rule, *Never eat anything red – but especially don't choose that colour for your cupcake frosting if your best friend can't stand strawberry*, even though I have to admit that the frosting was pretty good; it tasted more like vanilla with red food colouring in it than it did like strawberries, which I hate.

But still. The rule I broke was the more important one, the *Treat your friends the way you'd want them to treat you* rule. I certainly wouldn't want someone to shove a spatula down *my* throat – even if it was just a little. I pretty much deserved not to be Mary Kay's best friend any more. Especially since, clearly, I didn't know the first thing about the rules of friendship.

That is when it became clear to me that I needed to write them down. The rules, I mean. Because there are so many to remember that sometimes even I forget them. And I'm the one who's making them up.

So I found a spiral notebook in a box near the Christmas ornaments that Mom had marked SCHOOL SUPPLIES. Then, using one of her permanent markers that she saves for writing on her home-improvement tools and told us kids especially not to use (except that this was an emergency, so I knew she would understand), I wrote ALLIE FINKLE'S RULES FOR GIRLS across the front of it.

Then I wrote KEEP OUT IF YOU ARE NOT A GIRL (I wrote that because I have little brothers who are always butting into my business. I don't need them knowing my rules. They can make up their own rules if they're that interested).

I was sitting back in the wheelbarrow, writing out the rule about remembering to wear a helmet while skateboarding on High Street, when Carol surprised me by coming into the garage and asking me to come back to Mary Kay's house. She said Mary Kay was crying even harder because I'd left. Also, she said that I probably hadn't done any permanent damage to Mary Kay's uvula or tonsils.

I got out of the wheelbarrow and went back to

MOVING DAY

Mary Kay's, even though I didn't really want to. I did it because that's what friends do. When I got there, Mary Kay hugged me and told me she forgave me and that she knew I hadn't meant to hurt her.

I was glad Mary Kay had forgiven me, but secretly I felt a little mad too. Because of course I hadn't meant to hurt her. I swear, it's a total burden having a best friend who is as sensitive as Mary Kay. I always have to be super careful around her not to say or do the wrong thing (such as accidentally touch her uvula with a spatula) because Mary Kay is an only child and used to getting her way.

And if she doesn't get her own way, like if we're playing lions (her favourite game. NOT mine. My favourite game is detective. Not that we ever get to play it) and I say she should be the male lion for a change because I have rug burns from crawling around doing all the hunting, and I want to lie around with the cute cubs (even though in the wild the female lions do all the hunting, not the male lions, as I know from my extensive reading on animals), she just starts crying.

Or if I get to lick the spatula and she wants it.

Still, I showed her my notebook – the one in which I was writing the rules. I thought maybe if she saw the rules, she might actually try following them for a change, especially the *Treat your friends the way you'd want them to treat you* one.

First I made her swear not to tell anybody about it though. I explained to her that I was going to hide the notebook in a special place under the slats beneath my bed so my brothers wouldn't find it. I thought this actually might make her interested in reading it.

But it didn't. Mary Kay just yawned and asked if I wanted to play lions.

Which is too bad, because if anyone could use some help with the rules of friendship, it's Mary Kay.

I'm starting to think I could use a new best friend. A different, non-crying best friend. Just for a change.

It's kind of funny that I was thinking this, because when I got home from Mary Kay's that night, Mom and Dad told us we were moving.

Rule #2

Don't Get a Pet That Poops in Your Hand

It wasn't the hugest surprise that Mom and Dad said we were moving. Mom has been wanting a new house to test out her home-improvement skills for a while. Mom doesn't like our house because it doesn't need any home improvements. It's a contemporary split-level in Walnut Knolls, which is a housing development.

Mom wants an old falling-down Victorian house in town that she can restore to its former glory. She and Dad just bought an already finished house in a housing development because it was the only kind of house they could afford right after Dad got his teaching job.

My dad teaches college. What he teaches is computers.

Dad has been teaching computers for a while now

and recently got a chair. When you're a professor, getting a chair doesn't mean that you finally get to sit down at work. It means that you get more money. Also, my littlest brother, Kevin, started kindergarten, so Mom went back to work as an adviser. She advises college kids on what classes they should be taking (such as computer classes).

So we are getting more money because of that too.

Since both Mom and Dad will be at the college all day, they want to move closer to it – also to an old house, which Mom can have fun fixing up in her spare time from advising.

Only, I don't see what's so fun about fixing up an old house. I don't see what's wrong with staying in the house we have now, which doesn't need fixing up and has wall-to-wall cream-coloured carpeting, except in my room, where the carpeting is pink.

'But, Allie,' Mom said, trying to explain. 'The new house is so much bigger than this one. Mark and Kevin will be able to have their own rooms, so they won't fight as much. Won't that be nice?'

I know I am supposed to love my brothers, and I do. Like, I wouldn't want either of them to be hit by a car and have their brains splattered all over High Street.

Moving Day

But I don't particularly care if they have their own rooms.

'But what about my canopy bed?' I asked. Because I just got a canopy bed for *my* ninth birthday (I am older than Mary Kay by a month. Possibly this is why I don't cry as often as she does, because I am more mature. Also, I am more used to hardship, not being an only child).

'We'll take your canopy bed to the new house,' Dad explained. 'In the moving truck.'

My brother Mark was very excited to hear about the moving truck. Mark is in the second grade, and all he thinks about are trucks. Also, bugs.

'Can I ride in the moving truck?' he wanted to know. 'In the back, with all the furniture?'

'No,' Dad said. 'Because that is against the law.'

'The new house is much closer to where Dad and I work,' Mom went on. 'So we'll be able to spend more time with you kids because we won't have to drive so far to get to the office.'

'What about my rock collection?' I wanted to know. 'I have over two hundred of them now, you know.'

I know rocks might sound like a very boring thing to collect, but I select my rocks very carefully and keep them in paper grocery bags on my closet floor.

Each one of my rocks is, in its own way, extra-ordinary. Most of my rocks are geodes, which if you don't know, are very average-looking rocks – on the *outside*.

Inside, however, they have crystals that sparkle like diamonds. In fact, if you didn't know better, you might actually mistake a geode for a diamond.

You can't really tell just from looking at a rock whether it is an ordinary rock or a geode. Well, I mean, you can, but it takes practice.

Also, geodes are not easy to crack open to get to the crystals inside. To crack them open, you either have to throw them very hard against the sidewalk or driveway (which I would not recommend doing, because they leave marks on the driveway that some-times won't wash away for up to a year or more, as I found out the hard way) or hit them very hard with something metal, such as a hammer. I learned from experience that your dad's golf clubs are not very good for this.

I found most of my geodes while scavenging in the many home-construction sites in and around Walnut Knolls. Even though Mom and Dad say we're not supposed to go walking around construction sites, the truth is you can find many amazing things in the dirt piles bulldozers have made.

12

MOVING DAY

'Ten large grocery sacks of rocks,' Mom said, 'is simply too many, Allie. Especially considering the fact that you've never even cleaned your rocks, nor do you take very good care of them.'

'They're not rocks,' I informed her. 'They're geodes.'

'Whatever they are,' Mom said, 'they just sit in those sacks, cluttering up the floor of your closet. You can pick out three or four special rocks to take along. But the rest you're going to have to put back in the dirt where you found them.'

I couldn't help letting out a really disappointed cry at this. Because, seriously, I have put a lot of time and work into my rock collection. Sure, maybe I haven't cleaned them. But I love them, just the same.

But then an even worse thought hit me.

'What about school?' I asked. 'If the new house is close to your work, that means it must be really far from school. How are we going to be able to walk that far and still get to school on time?'

'Well,' Mom said, 'you'll be going to a new school, because we'll be living in a different school district. But Pine Heights Elementary is right around the corner from the new house. In fact, you'll be able to walk home for lunch if you want to! Won't that be fun?'

But I didn't think that sounded fun at all. I thought that sounded terrible, actually.

'I don't want to go to a new school!' I cried. Really cried, on account of, well, I was crying. I may cry less often than Mary Kay does. But I still cry sometimes. 'What about Ms Myers?'

Ms Myers is my teacher. She is the best teacher I ever had. She has hair that is so long she can sit on it.

'I'm sure you'll love your new teacher too,' Mom said. 'We'll go over and meet all your new teachers before you start at the new school, so you'll get a chance to know them. How does that sound?'

'That sounds good to me,' Mark said, chewing. He was eating fish fingers with ketchup, despite my advising him never to eat anything red.

Mark, it was clear, didn't care about moving – except whether or not he got to ride in the back of the moving truck with the furniture. He didn't care about having to start a whole new school and make all new friends.

'Shut up,' I said to Mark.

'Don't tell your brother to shut up,' Dad said. When Dad tells you not to do something, you stop doing it. That is also a rule – and one Mark and Kevin actually follow.

Moving Day

But still.

'What about Mary Kay?' All of a sudden I remembered my best friend. Only I didn't remember the part about how I'd just been sort of wishing for a different, non-crying best friend. 'If we move, I won't be in the same class with her any more! I won't live down the street from her any more!'

'You can still go visit her,' my little brother Kevin said helpfully. 'You can take the bus.'

'I don't want to take the bus!' I screamed.

'Stop screaming,' Dad said. 'Nobody's going to be taking any buses. Allie, you'll still see your friend. Just not at school. You can have whatever-they're-called.'

'Play dates,' Mom said. 'Your father means we'll organize play dates with Mary Kay.'

Play dates? Whatever! I don't want to organize 'play dates' with Mary Kay. Mary Kay and I have never had to organize 'play dates' before. Whenever Mary Kay and I want to play, I just walk down the street and we play together. There's no *organizing* anything.

'I don't want to move!' I cried. 'I don't want to give up my rock collection, or go to a new school, or organize play dates with Mary Kay! I want to stay right here!'

'Allie,' Mom said. 'Your father and I were thinking. If you can show you can be grown-up about this move and give it a try and not cry about it, we might decide you're old enough to have a pet of your own.'

I was so shocked, I stopped crying. I have always wanted a pet of my own. We have Marvin, of course, and I love him very much. For instance, I am the only person in my family who brushes him, checks him for ticks and walks him (well, Dad walks him too, but only at night). I want to be a vet when I grow up, so I am also practising for when this happens.

But I have always wanted a pet of my very own, one I wouldn't have to share with everyone else, such as my brothers.

'You mean,' I said, sniffling, 'I could have a hamster, like Mary Kay?'

'No hamsters,' my dad said. Dad doesn't like hamsters or even mice. The time Mary Kay and I caught a baby mouse in the field behind her house (where they are now building a new development) and put it in my Polly Pocket Pollywood Limo-Scene, then showed it to my dad, he made us let it go in the woods behind our house (where they are also now building a new development), even though we explained to him it would probably die without us or its mother to take care of it.

MOVING DAY

Dad didn't care. He says he doesn't like animals that don't know any better than to poop in your hand.

So when I wrote that down it became the rule of: *Don't get a pet that poops in your hand.*

'Actually,' Mom said, 'we were thinking you might be old enough now to take care of your own kitten.'

I didn't think I heard her right. Had she said . . . KITTEN?

'No fair!' Mark yelled. 'I want a kitten!'

'Me too!' Kevin yelled.

She did. She *did* say kitten! How had they known? How had they known I'd been wanting a kitten for my whole life, practically?

And true, I had asked for a miniature poodle for my birthday and gotten a canopy bed instead, which isn't as good.

But it had never even occurred to me to ask for a kitten.

Until they said I could have one.

And then I knew I wanted a kitten more than I had ever wanted anything in my entire life. Kittens are way better than hamsters, who, by the way, poop in your hand.

'When you guys show that you can be grown-up enough to handle the responsibility of having your own pet,' Dad said to my brothers, 'we'll talk. But I haven't seen either of you brushing Marvin, or taking him on walks the way Allie does.'

'I take Marvin on walks,' Mark said.

'Hitching Marvin up to the sled and trying to make him pull you down the dirt piles in the new development does not count as walking him,' Mom pointed out to Mark. 'Now, who wants to go to Dairy Queen as a treat for dessert?'

We all wanted to go to Dairy Queen, of course.

To get to the Dairy Queen from our house, you have to drive in the car. It was while we were in the car driving to Dairy Queen that Mom said, 'You know, the new house is so close to the Dairy Queen that we could walk there after supper.'

'Like, for dessert?' Mark asked. This is another thing Mark thinks about all the time. Bugs, trucks and dessert.

Also, sports. Such as football. Or anything with a ball really.

'Right,' Mom said. 'After dinner. We could just get up and take a walk to Dairy Queen.'

We all – Mark, Kevin and I – looked at each other in astonishment. Walk to Dairy Queen? Every night?

This was almost too much to believe. A kitten *and* Dairy Queen? *Every* night?

MOVING DAY

'*If* you guys finish everything on your plates,' Dad added.

'Maybe,' Mom said slowly, 'we could drive by and see the new house tonight. On our way back from Dairy Queen.'

'I don't know,' Dad said. 'I don't think these kids are really that interested in seeing the new house.'

'*I* am,' Mark said, leaning forward in his seat. '*I'm* interested in seeing the new house.'

'I want to see the new house too,' Kevin said.

'How about you, Allie?' Mom asked. 'Are you interested in seeing the new house too?'

I had to think about that. On the one hand, I was interested in a new kitten. I was interested in Dairy Queen every night and in getting a new best friend.

On the other hand, I was not interested in starting a new school or in getting rid of my rock collection.

Still, if the new house was really that close to Dairy Queen . . .

'Well,' I said. 'I guess it wouldn't hurt to *see* it . . .'

It didn't seem like the Dairy Queen people could make our ice-cream cones fast enough. It seemed like it took them *forever*. And all we got was our usuals – chocolate-vanilla twist chocolate dip for me, vanilla twist cherry dip for Mark and vanilla twist butterscotch dip for Kevin, a diet root-beer float for Dad and a sugar-free Dilly Bar for Mom.

Still, it seemed like it took *two hours* for them to get our order ready, and for Dad to pay, and for Mom to get enough napkins from the dispenser in case somebody spilled in the car (I said somebody, but Mark is always the one who spills, usually all down the front of his shirt), and for everyone to get back in the car and to get their seat belts on without spilling, and for Dad to go, 'Is everybody ready? Does anybody want to drive by the new house?' and for us all to go, 'YES!' and for him to go, 'OK! Here we go.'

And then we were turning around the corner – right around the corner! That's really where the new house was, right around the corner from the Dairy Queen – and Mom was going, in an excited voice, 'There it is, kids, there it is, right there on the left, see it? See it?'

And we all looked at the new place where we were going to live.

And I don't know about everyone else, but I for one nearly threw up what I'd eaten so far of my ice cream.

Because the new house was not very nice-looking.

In fact, it looked the opposite of nice. It looked very big and creepy sitting there on the street. All the windows – and there were a lot of them – were dark and sort of looked like eyes staring down at us. There were a lot of big trees around the house too, with twisted branches that were swaying in the wind.

There are no big trees in Walnut Knolls. That's because only nine years ago, when I was born, Walnut Knolls was all fields and farmland. None of the trees the developers planted have had a chance to grow much yet.

'Mom,' I said.

'Isn't it *great*?' Mom said, all excitedly. 'Look at the gingerbread trim around the front porch! And how exciting is the fact that we even have a front porch where we can sit outside and enjoy the summer breeze?'

'And have ice cream,' Mark said. 'Right? We can sit out there and enjoy ice cream.' Because ice cream is all Mark thinks about. Besides bugs and trucks and sports.

'We sure can,' Mom said. 'And see that bay window on the third floor in the front? That'll be your room, Allie.'

My room looked darkest and creepiest of all.

'Those trees sure are big,' Kevin said.

'Those trees,' Mom said, 'are over a hundred years old. Just like the house.'

Which, looking at it through the car window, I could totally believe. Our new house looked more than a hundred years old. It looked so old that it was falling apart, practically. It looked like all those houses on those TV shows my mom likes to watch, TV shows called things such as *Please Come Fix Up My House* and *My House Is Really Old. Won't Someone Fix It, Please?*

Only this wasn't a TV show. This was real life. And no nice team of carpenters and pretty designers was going to come and fix it up. My mom was going to have to fix up our house – with Dad's help, I guess – herself.

I don't mean to sound like a spoilsport, but the truth is, I really didn't think she was going to be able to do it.

Because the house we were sitting in front of looked beyond fixing.

Also, the house we were sitting in front of looked something else. I didn't want to mention it in front of Mark and Kevin, because one of the rules – which I was going to write down as soon as I got home – is that *You shouldn't scare your little brothers* (unless they've done something to deserve it, of course).

But the truth was, that house looked haunted to me.

22

Moving Day

Suddenly I didn't want my ice cream any more.

Also, I was pretty sure I didn't want to move any more, even if it *did* mean Dairy Queen every night, a new, possibly non-crying best friend and a kitten.

Instead, I wanted everything back the way it was, before Mom and Dad said I could have a kitten, before they said we were moving and before I'd accidentally touched my best friend's uvula with a spatula.

Only that turns out to be one of the hardest rules to learn of all: *You can't go back.*

But even though you can't go back, you *can* keep things from changing more. If you try hard enough.

And I knew then that that was what I had to do.

I just didn't know how. Yet.

Rule #3

If You Don't Want a Secret Spread Around, Don't Tell It to Scott Stamphley

Mary Kay cried when I told her that it looked like we were moving. Which I guess was no big surprise, since Mary Kay cries about everything.

Except that this was one of the few times I actually felt like crying with her.

'You can't move *now*,' Mary Kay said. 'It's the middle of the school year. It's against the rules.'

There's a lot of stuff I don't know about – like friendship and fixing up old haunted houses, for example.

But one thing I do know about is rules.

'I'm sure that's not true,' I said. 'Because if it was my mom and dad wouldn't be making us do it.'

'Well,' Mary Kay said, 'you'd better make sure they check. Because this new school might not even let you in in the middle of the semester like this.'

Moving Day

That's the other thing about Mary Kay. She kind of thinks she knows everything.

'Well,' I said, 'Mom said if we move, we *have* to go to this new school because we'll be living in a new school district. So I don't think I have much of a choice.'

'You make it sound like you want to move,' Mary Kay said, all accusingly.

'Of course I don't want to move,' I said. I hadn't even told her the part about the house maybe possibly being haunted. But I did tell her the part about the kitten.

This just made her cry harder. Which didn't make any sense at all. I mean, you would have thought she'd have been a *little* happy for me on account of the kitten.

Except that she wasn't.

'You know if you get a kitten I won't be able to come over,' she said through her tears as we waited for the crossing guard, Mrs Mullens, to let us cross High Street. 'I'm allergic to cats!'

'You never come over anyway,' I pointed out. We always play at Mary Kay's house, because she says my brothers are too rough. All because one time when she came over to my house and we were playing lions (the only game Mary Kay will *ever* play), Mark decided he was a killer lion from a rival pride and pounced on Mary Kay from the coffee table. Not surprisingly, this made her cry.

'Yes,' Mary Kay said. 'But now I *really* won't.'

'It will be OK,' I said, to reassure her. 'I'll come see you.'

'No you won't,' Mary Kay said, still crying. 'You'll be too busy with your new friends and your k-kitten!'

I knew this was probably true but I didn't say so, because one of the rules of friendship that I wrote down is *You should only say nice things to your friends, even if they're not true.* This makes them feel better, and then they like you more.

Being liked is important. If no one likes you, then you have to eat lunch by yourself, like Scott Stamphley did when he first came to our school and no one could understand anything he said because of his New York accent.

'I'll never be too busy for you, Mary Kay,' I said as nicely as I could, considering how mad she was making me. 'Although raising a kitten is a lot of responsibility. More responsibility than raising a hamster.'

'No it isn't,' Mary Kay said.

'Yes,' I said to her. 'It really is.'

Moving Day

'I don't think you should be so happy about moving,' Mary Kay said. 'Because, first of all, if you move it means you won't be able to walk to school with me any more.'

I just looked at her when she said this, because walking to school with Mary Kay isn't actually all that much fun. She is so afraid of everything that if Buck – that's the name of the horse who grazes in the last field that's left in Walnut Knolls (without houses being built on it, I mean), and which also happens to be right next to the sidewalk we take to school – has his head over the fence, she runs away. She's scared of Buck's huge teeth, even though I showed her how to hold her hand flat so Buck's teeth can't nip her palm when we give him leftover Fruit Roll-Ups from our lunches or whatever.

You have to know about these things if you are going to be a vet.

But, remembering the rule about only saying nice things to your friends so they'll like you, I said, 'Well, that *will* make me sad. But I'll probably get used to it. Eventually.'

Apparently this answer wasn't good enough for Mary Kay though, because she added, 'And also, if you move, you won't be able to look for that kid's brain in the bushes any more.'

Which I didn't think was a very nice thing for her to point out. Especially since she knows how much I want to find that kid's brain.

And it wasn't as if I wasn't already freaking out about maybe having to move into a haunted house and start at a whole new school. I mean, except for the part about the kitten – and maybe getting a better best friend than Mary Kay – I didn't even want to move.

But I still didn't know what I was supposed to do about it. It wasn't like I had a choice about moving. I was just a kid!

'Look,' I said to Mary Kay, 'let's not fight. I'll probably be moving in a few weeks, so let's try to get along until then.'

'Quit saying that!' cried Mary Kay. 'Quit saying you're moving! It's my birthday! I don't want you to say you're moving ONE MORE TIME TODAY.'

I felt even worse after that. I'd totally forgotten it was Mary Kay's birthday . . . even though I should have remembered, since Carol was coming to school later with the pink-frosting cupcakes.

So I promised not to tell anyone that I might be moving for the rest of the day.

And I didn't. I didn't tell anyone at all that I might be moving, not even Ms Myers when she told us we

28

needed to pick a country that we would be studying individually for the rest of the year for our data reports. I didn't say to her, 'Well, Ms Myers, you see, that will be a problem, because I might not be here any more after next month.'

I didn't tell Brittany Hauser I might be moving when she asked if I wanted to come over to her house to see the fancy show cat her dad bought her mom as an anniversary surprise.

I didn't tell Mrs Fleener, the lunchroom lady, that I might be moving when she told me to remind my mother that she hadn't paid for my lunch milk for next month.

I didn't tell anyone at all that I might be moving.

At least until somehow I ended up standing next to Scott Stamphley during dodgeball in PE (which we were only playing because it was raining and so we couldn't go outside to play baseball).

And the truth is, by then I was bursting to tell *someone*. And I figured it would be safe to tell Scott, since no girls in my class will talk to him. Not because of his New York accent. We all got over that after the first few days of meeting him. But because of his snake collection, which he insists on bringing to school every time there is a science fair. So it wasn't like there was anyone he could tell anyway.

'Want to know a secret?' I asked him as we stood in the back where the big red balls couldn't get us. Mary Kay was already out – she'd gotten hit by a ball first thing, because of course everyone wanted to strike her out on her birthday and make her cry. Which completely worked. So now she was sitting on the sidelines showing Mr Phelps the red mark from the ball on her thigh and saying, 'B-but it's m-my b-birthday!' between sobs.

'Not really,' Scott said, about my secret question.

But since I know he was just saying that to be a pain, I told him anyway. 'I'm probably moving.'

'Big deal,' Scott said. Which is one of the reasons why no girls like him. Because he is so rude to us. Also because he does things like burp loudly in class when Ms Myers isn't paying attention, which Brittany Hauser says is disgusting.

But I didn't care that he was being rude to me because it was just such a relief to tell someone.

'I probably won't be going to this school any more,' I told him.

'Good,' Scott said. 'Then I won't have to look at your stupid face any more.'

Since this is just the way Scott is, I didn't take offence. Also because I know if you gasp and flounce away when boys act like this, like Brittany Hauser does, you are really just giving them what they want.

'It's going to be really hard,' I told him. 'I'll have to make all new friends.'

'That *is* going to be really hard for you,' Scott said. 'On account of how ugly you are.'

If Scott had said that to Mary Kay, of course she would have started crying. But I'm used to the way boys talk because of my brothers.

So I said, 'Look at this bruise I got falling off my bike.' And I showed him this huge green-and-blue bruise on my elbow, which doesn't hurt but is very disgusting-looking.

And Scott, just like I'd known he would, leaned in real close to look at it, going, '*Sweet . . .*'

And that's when I jumped out of the way and, like, thirty balls hit him in the face.

Yesssssss. Talk about sweet.

But I guess Scott didn't think it was so sweet, because later, as Carol came into our class holding all the cupcakes, Mary Kay walked up to me, crying, and said, 'Thanks a lot for ruining my birthday!'

I was totally shocked. I couldn't see how I'd ruined Mary Kay's birthday, since I hadn't been doing anything but colouring in a picture of a lion, which I'd planned on presenting her *for* her birthday.

'What do you mean?' I asked her.

'Why don't you just ask Scott?' she said, and flounced away.

I looked over at Scott and saw that he was making a *giant* card for Mary Kay, which said, *Too bad Allie's moving, now you'll have no friends at all. Happy Birthday!*

And a second later, Brittany Hauser and her best friend, Courtney Wilcox, came up to me and were, like, 'You're moving? How come you didn't tell us?' right as Carol and Ms Myers starting singing 'Happy Birthday'.

But the birthday girl had already put her head down on her desk and was crying.

So I guess it wasn't a very happy birthday for her after all.

Rule #4

Brothers – and Parents – Can Be
Very Insensitive

The good part about being in a fight with my best friend was that it was going to make moving away from her much easier. For instance, now I wouldn't have to worry about setting up 'play dates' with her after we moved, or about buying her a going-away present, such as one half of a locket and myself the other half so we'd each have half a locket to remember the other person by (I saw that in a movie once).

But the bad part about having a fight with my best friend was that I didn't have anyone to talk to about how upset I was about the actual moving thing. Because even though I was trying not to show it, because I didn't want to upset my little brothers, I was really, really upset, especially after Mom and Dad signed all the papers and finally got the keys to the new house. Because that's when we went from 'maybe' moving to 'definitely' moving. Also when they took us over there for our first big tour, I couldn't believe what I saw. I mean, if I'd thought the front of our new house was scary-looking, well, that was nothing compared to how scary it turned out to be on the *inside*.

Because it was way worse than anything I'd ever seen on any episode of *Please Come Fix Up My House*.

In fact, if you ask me, Mom and Dad could not have picked a gloomier, more depressing place to live in.

Well, maybe if they had picked the haunted house that Uncle Jay took me to at the county fair last summer. But that might actually have been nicer than the house we were supposedly going to live in.

Because at least the county-fair haunted house had bowls of grape eyeballs and spaghetti-noodle guts you could stick your hands in.

But our new house didn't have any gross-yet-cool stuff like that. Instead, it had these walls that were painted some sort of dark grey (which Mom said she was going to paint over. Like *that* was going to make a difference) except where the people who owned the house before us had hung their paintings. There, the walls had these rectangular patches of brown.

And the house had these ceilings that swooped up

forever that Mom kept going on all excitedly about. 'Twelve-foot ceilings!' she kept saying, but I didn't see what was so great about them. They just ended up in these cobwebby chandeliers that weren't even a bit sparkly like my geodes.

And even though Mom kept going, 'And just *look* at these magnificent wood floors,' the truth was, the wall-to-wall carpeting back at our old house was way nicer, if you ask me, than the nasty dark brown wood floors that we were walking on that went *creeeeaak* when you stepped anywhere on them.

As if all that wasn't bad enough, there were spiders *everywhere*, not just in the basement. And every room was colder than the last one. The whole place felt as if no one had lived in it for at least a hundred years.

But that wasn't the worst of it. The worst of it was my room – the one Mom had pointed out from the car on Dairy Queen night. Because it turned out to be the coldest, darkest room of all. And the floor in there was also the creakiest – whoever heard of a bedroom that wasn't even carpeted? And even though it had what Mom called a bay window that was like a turret in a castle that was round and almost all glass that she said Dad was going to build a window seat in that I'd be able to sit on and read my books, you couldn't even see the town electrical tower from the windows, just trees and the tops of other people's houses.

How was I going to be able to fall asleep at night if I couldn't see the red light from the electrical tower blinking on and off, on and off, warning aeroplanes not to fly into it?

How?

When I asked Dad about that, he just went, 'Well, Allie, you're just going to have to learn to fall asleep a different way.'

Like that was even *possible*.

As I stood there in the giant echoing cavern that was supposed to be my room, I couldn't help remembering what had happened the night before. And that was that our estate agent, Mrs Klinghoffer, had come over and put a big FOR SALE sign in the front yard of our perfectly nice, non-creaky, non-haunted split-level that for some reason my parents wanted to move away from.

Mrs Klinghoffer had brushed her hands together all satisfied when she was done planting the sign and looked at me staring at her from the dirt pile that will soon become the house behind ours, where I was digging for more geodes to add to my rock collection (which I will soon have to throw away). She'd smiled and then she'd said, 'Don't worry, Allie. This sign won't be here long. Your old house will sell in no time.'

I know it's a rule that *You're not supposed to hate people, especially grown-up people*. I know it's a rule because I wrote it down in my book of rules right after Mrs Klinghoffer drove away.

But the truth is, I'd sort of hated Mrs Klinghoffer right then.

And the thing was, Mrs Klinghoffer had been totally wrong. I hadn't been worrying about our house not selling. What I had been worrying about was somebody buying our house before Mom and Dad had time to realize what a horrible mistake they were making selling it in the first place.

But I guess I was the only person in our family who thought that. Even Mark and Kevin didn't agree with me about our new house stinking. I could tell by the way I could hear them crying, 'Sweet!' and 'Cool!' over their new rooms across the hall from mine.

And it wasn't just that they each finally had their own rooms and didn't have to share. They actually seemed to love their horrible, dark, boxlike rooms at the top of the third floor (all the kids' rooms in the new house were on a floor by themselves, sharing one bathroom – that, by the way, was really old-fashioned with a bathtub that had feet on it and spiders in the drain).

The reason Mark and Kevin loved their new rooms (besides the fact that they didn't have to share any more) was because there was a heating grate in the wall that separated their two rooms and they'd figured out that they could open the grate up and talk to each other through it. And when they did that, their voices sounded all weird, like they were communicating from outer space or something. They'd already made up a new game: space shuttle. The game went like this: one person sat on one side of the grate and the other person sat on the other, each in his own room. Then each person opened the grate on his side.

Then one person went, into the grate: 'Houston, Houston, this is the space shuttle. Do you read me? Over.'

Then the other person went, into the grate: 'Space shuttle, space shuttle, this is Houston, we read you. Over.'

Then the other person went: 'Houston, we have a problem. Repeat. We have a problem. Thrusters are ON FIRE. Repeat. Thrusters are ON FIRE. Over.'

And so on.

Yes, it was stupid. But what can you expect?

MOVING DAY

They're little brothers. It doesn't take much to make them happy.

Mark and Kevin didn't see the huge problems ahead – that this house was too big and too broken-down for Mom, even with Dad's help, to fix by herself, especially without the help of a TV carpenter or pretty designer. That we were going to have to switch to a whole new school in the middle of the year. That we were going to have to leave behind not just our rock collections – those of us who had them – but our best friends.

And OK, maybe our best friends hadn't been the greatest, but they'd still been our best friends, who were, strictly speaking, better than no best friends. You don't come across a best friend – even not-so-great ones – every day. Best friends are actually hard to find. Even the kind who aren't actually speaking to you at the moment.

Mom and Dad were asking us to give up all this and for what? Dairy Queen every night? A kitten? To move to a broken-down, possibly haunted house from which we couldn't even see the electrical tower? It was so unfair!

Besides, Mark and Kevin were too young to see what Mom and Dad were doing: sticking us kids up at the top of the house – well, as close to the top as we could be, apart from the attic, which you could reach by a trapdoor in the ceiling of the hallway between our three rooms. Yes, really, a trapdoor, which you pulled down with a cord – on purpose so that they could Be Alone and Get Away From Us Kids.

Mom and Dad claimed this wasn't true, of course. But when I accused them of it, I caught them smiling a little. Then they said, 'Now, Allie . . . have you given any thought to the kind of kitten you want?'

They may think just because I'm nine I can't see through what they're doing – trying to change the subject of wanting to stick us kids on a floor by ourselves so they can be alone.

But I can see that that is *exactly* what they're doing.

And all I can say is that when we finally move in and something (such as a disembodied zombie hand) comes crawling out of that attic to get us (I saw this happen in a movie once) and our screams pierce the night, and Mom and Dad have to come running up all those twisty stairs to get to us, well, they deserve what they find when they finally reach our bloodied and lifeless bodies.

Mom could see that I wasn't too happy about the situation and that no amount of kitten talk was going to change things.

So she tried to make it better by going, 'You know, you kids are going to get to be in charge of picking out your own paint colour or wallpaper for your rooms.'

'Really?' Mark said. 'Like, I can have wallpaper with trucks all over it? Or bugs?'

'Anything you want,' Mom said.

'Cool,' Kevin said. 'I'm getting purple velvet wallpaper, just like at Lung Chung, the Chinese food restaurant.'

'Anything you want within reason,' Mom corrected herself. 'Wouldn't you rather have nice sailboat wallpaper, Kevin?'

'No,' Kevin said.

'What about pirate ships?' Dad suggested.

'If they're velvet pirate ships,' Kevin said.

'I want pink-rose wallpaper,' I said. 'And pink wall-to-wall carpeting.'

'But, Allie,' Mom said, 'that's what you have in your room in the old house.'

'Exactly,' I said firmly.

'But where's the fun in that?' Mom wanted to know. 'Don't you want to try new things?'

'I do,' Kevin said. 'I want to try velvet.'

'Why don't you kids go outside to play for a while?' Dad said.

'Right,' Mom said. 'Dad and I just have to do a little more measuring, then we'll be ready to leave.'

Mark and Kevin groaned. They didn't want to go outside. They liked playing inside the new house, not just because of the heating grate but because it has all these long hallways and secret passageways to play in (no, really: the house has these back staircases and rooms for the servants to use – back in the olden times when people had maids and stuff).

My brothers didn't mind that the long hallways were dark and creepy and the secret passageways smelled like the inside of Scott Stamphley's shoe that he dared me to sniff after PE one time.

The reason my brothers didn't mind about this was because brothers are not very sensitive. Kind of like parents.

That is a rule that I have to remember to write down by the way: *Brothers and parents aren't very sensitive*. I don't mean that they aren't very sensitive like Mary Kay, who cries all the time. I mean that, a lot of the time, little brothers just don't *get* stuff. Like that long creepy hallways aren't fun to play in and that our parents are sticking us up on the third floor to get rid of us.

I, on the other hand, hurried to take Mom's suggestion and rushed outside, even though it was autumn and so getting kind of cold out, also dark earlier and earlier. I would have done anything to get out of that crummy house, even stand in the cold and dark waiting for Mom and Dad to get done measuring.

That's how much I hated our new house.

The house had a pretty big backyard, but there was no swing set or anything to play on back there. Just trees and yard. And there were no geodes that I could find and use to start a new rock collection after my current one got thrown out. There was nothing in our new yard but some bald patches where there used to be grass.

But there was one tree that had branches low enough that you could climb them. So Mark and Kevin started climbing.

'Come on, Allie,' Mark called to me from the lower branches (which were sagging beneath his weight). 'Climb with us.'

'You're so dumb,' I said to him, in a spurt of disbelief over his insensitivity. 'Can't you see what's happening?'

'No,' he said. 'Except that you're in a bad mood.'

'Mom and Dad are making a huge mistake buying this new house,' I informed him.

'I like the new house,' Kevin said. 'I'm going to get velvet wallpaper just like at Lung Chung.'

While Lung Chung is Kevin's favourite restaurant because it is very fancy, and Kevin likes fancy things, it's not my favourite. Because in addition to having velvet wallpaper, it also serves turtle soup. It even keeps a turtle in a big plastic pond – with its own island to sit on – on the floor inside the door when you walk in.

So far no one in our town has ever ordered turtle soup. I know, because I check the turtle every time we go there, and it's always been there.

But you never know. Someone could order the turtle soup any day. And when that day comes, the turtle will be gone. This is cruelty to animals, if you ask me.

Thinking about that turtle always makes me mad.

'Mom already said you couldn't have velvet wallpaper,' I pointed out.

'No, she didn't,' Kevin said. 'She said I could get velvet *pirate* wallpaper.'

'There's no such thing, Kevin.'

'Yes, there is. And I'm going to get a lamp like they have on all the tables at Lung Chung too.'

'You can't have a red stained-glass lamp in your *bedroom*, stupid.'

'Yes, I can,' Kevin said. 'And *you're* stupid not to like this house. This house is the *best*.'

'No, it's not,' I said. Maybe it was because I was

thinking about that turtle at Lung Chung. Or maybe it was just because I was thinking about our house. In any case, suddenly, I was really, really mad. 'It's dark and cold and ugly.'

Mark said, 'You know what, Allie? *You're* ugly. Hey – I'm telling! Then you're not going to get your kitten!'

I didn't care though. I didn't care if he told on me for punching him. Because I didn't punch him that hard, for one thing, and it was only on the foot anyway, the only part of him I could reach with him in the tree.

It doesn't count if it doesn't hurt. That's a rule.

Or it would be when I got home and wrote it down.

So I turned my back on them – even though I guess technically I was sort of supposed to be keeping an eye on them – and walked down the alley (there's an alley between our new house and the house next door) to the front yard and was standing there feeling ugly – as ugly as Mark had accused me of looking – when I heard voices and looked over to the house next door and noticed something I hadn't seen before.

And that was that there was a girl about my own age doing back handsprings in the front yard of her own house.

Rule #5

You Can't Let Your Family Move
into a Haunted House

Not only was there a girl my age doing back hand-springs in her front yard, but there was an older girl there as well, tossing a baton – a real one, like the kind majorettes in parades on TV use – in the air and actually *catching it as it came down.*

At first I kind of just stood there staring at them because they were the only forms of life I'd seen in our new neighbourhood the whole time we'd been there. All the houses on our new street were just like ours – big and scary-looking with lots of turrets and windows and yards surrounded by tall hedges and old trees with creepy branches – and so I just assumed old people lived in all of them.

But now I saw that some actual young people lived in one of them.

And not just young people but girls who could do

back handsprings and toss – *and actually catch* – a baton.

The girl who was doing back handsprings was really good at them. She had obviously been doing gymnastics for a very long time because she was quite sproingy. She was sproinging all over the yard.

I have never been able to do gymnastics. I have been taking ballet for two years. I kept on with it even after Mary Kay quit because Madame Linda never chose her to wear the tiara during cooldown. Before ballet, Mary Kay made me try tap lessons with her (hideous) and then gymnastics (even more hideous). My dad says quitters never win, but I say quitters *always* win, because when you quit things you end up making more time for finding out the things you love, such as rock-collecting.

But I didn't quit ballet. There is only one thing I like better than ballet, and that's baseball, which is a good sport because you get to hit a ball with a bat. The harder you hit it the better.

But unfortunately you don't get to hit the ball all the time. There is also the boring wait-until-it's-your-turn-to-hit-the-ball part.

This is like ballet. The best part of ballet is the grand jeté. This is when you run and leap – as high as you can go with your legs spread far apart, like you're flying, almost – into the air.

The worst part of ballet is anything to do with the barre, which is this thing they make you hold on to while you do pliés and stuff, which are a warm-up to the grand jeté.

I don't mind when I swing my bat and I don't hit the ball.

And I don't mind when Madame Linda doesn't think my grand jetés are the best in the class and so she lets someone else wear her tiara during cooldown.

What I do mind is when people try to make me do things I don't want to do. Such as move when I don't feel like moving. Or do gymnastics when my body just isn't very sproingy.

Not like the girl who was doing the back handsprings in her front yard. Her body was very, very sproingy.

Then I noticed that the girl who'd been doing the back handsprings had stopped doing them. Instead, she was standing up and staring at me over the hedge that surrounded her front yard and separated her yard from the alley between our houses.

'Hey,' the girl said, looking right at me. She had a big smile on her face. 'Hi. Are you the new girl?'

Moving Day

I almost looked over my shoulder to see who she was talking to. Because, the new girl? That sure wasn't me. I'm Allie Finkle. I'm not the new girl.

Then I remembered where I was.

And I remembered that, here, I *am* the new girl.

'Oh,' I said. 'Hi. Yes. I'm Allie Finkle.'

'I'm Erica Harrington,' the girl said. She was smiling like crazy. It was hard to imagine her crying just because someone said she wanted to be the girl lion for a change. 'And this is my sister, Missy.'

'Melissa,' the older girl with the baton corrected her, not in a very friendly way. She hadn't stopped throwing the baton in the air and catching it. She was really very good at it. As good as Erica was at gymnastics.

'I'm in fourth grade at Pine Heights Elementary,' Erica went on, not even stopping to admire how good her sister was at baton throwing and catching. Which I guess would be natural if you saw that kind of thing every day. 'Missy is in sixth grade over at the middle school. What about you?'

'I'm in fourth grade too,' I said. I was beginning to feel less sad than I'd felt before, when I'd been in the backyard and inside our terrible new house. In fact, I was beginning to feel a little – just a little – excited. I was beginning to feel excited because I was figuring something out. I was figuring out that Erica was the same age as me, and might – just might – end up being my new best friend.

I know it was too early to tell and everything. But, I mean, she lived next door to me and was in my same grade.

The thing was, she looked like she'd be so much better a best friend than Mary Kay, at least so far. She could do flawless back handsprings, had a sister in middle school who could toss *and* catch a baton, and she had shown no sign of crying during a nearly two-minute conversation.

Which was practically a world record as far as I was concerned.

But I really didn't want to get my hopes up because the whole day had already been such a big disappointment, what with the house and my room and everything. I mean, chances were a girl like Erica already had a best friend, anyway. I knew I shouldn't let myself get too excited.

'I go to Walnut Knolls Elementary,' I said, trying to stay calm but already tripping over my words a little in my haste to get them out. 'Only, I'll be starting at Pine Heights Elementary next month after we move in.'

MOVING DAY

Erica let out a polite scream to show she was excited too.

'Maybe we'll be in the same class,' she yelled. 'Do you know who your teacher is going to be? Because there are two fourth-grade classes at Pine Heights. There's Mrs Danielson. She's nice. But there's also my teacher, Mrs Hunter. She's *really* nice. I hope you're in my class!'

'I hope I'm in your class too!' I yelled back. I yelled because Erica yelled. *If someone is yelling from excitement, the polite thing to do is to yell back.* That's a rule. Or it would be when I got home.

'Stop all that yelling,' Melissa said. 'You're giving me a headache.'

'Oh,' I said, careful not to yell any more. 'Sorry.' To Erica, I said, 'Do you like kittens? Because I'm getting one.'

'I LOVE KITTENS!' Erica yelled. 'What kind are you getting?'

'Well,' I said, because I had been doing a lot of research on this ever since my parents said I could have one. 'The breed really doesn't matter to me, although I love Persians because they're really fluffy, and I love fluffy cats. The important thing to me, though, is that I get a rescued kitten because there are so many strays that need homes. So I'll probably get whatever they have at the ASPCA when we go to look.'

'Our cat, Polly, is from the ASPCA,' Erica shouted. 'Do you want to come inside and meet her? And see my dollhouse?'

'I'd love to meet your cat and see your dollhouse,' I shouted back.

'I said stop that yelling,' Melissa said. 'And don't you need to tell your parents where you're going first?'

'Oh, no,' I said. 'They don't care. Sorry about the yelling.'

And that's how I got to be friends with Erica from next door at the new house.

I'm not saying we were *best* friends, of course. Nothing like that! I mean, nobody mentioned anything about being best friends. I'm sure a girl like Erica has tons of friends, and maybe even three or four best friends. Who knows? It was fun just to be with her. Her house was almost exactly like our new house, only instead of being gloomy and depressing, Erica's house was extremely cheerful and welcoming. That was because her parents had already done a really great job fixing their house up, so instead of grey paint on the walls there was pretty cream-coloured wallpaper with tiny rosebuds on it.

Moving Day

And instead of the floors being dark brown, they were light brown and shiny, and they didn't creak – or at least not in a bad way. And the chandeliers were sparkly and actually lit up when you turned them on, as opposed to the chandeliers in our house, which did nothing when you turned them on.

Erica introduced me to her cat, Polly, who was a beautiful calico who only hissed at me once. Then she showed me a funny button that you can press under the carpet in the dining room that rings a bell in one of the secret passageways by the kitchen. In olden times, that was to alert the cook that the family was ready for the next course to be served, like the salad course or whatever.

Erica and I had fun pressing the button until her mom came out and said if we went to play with Erica's dollhouse she'd make us some hot chocolate.

So we went up to Erica's room, which was just like my room in the new house, but fixed up all nice and pretty, with pink carpeting and a canopy bed like in my room back home.

Only Erica's room wasn't scary or depressing at all!

And in the turret part of Erica's room sat this huge dollhouse – as tall as me – that Erica said had been in her family since her grandma's days and that had lights you could really turn on and even actual running water so the dollhouse people could take a bath (except they couldn't really because they were made of felt, and they'd melt if you put them in the water).

It was the nicest, fanciest dollhouse I'd ever seen. Kevin would have died of joy.

And best of all, Erica didn't cry when I asked if I could be the girl doll. She didn't even sniffle. She went, in a perfectly cheerful manner, 'OK. I'll be the mother doll.'

And then, later, when I suggested that the baby doll get kidnapped and a ransom note, including the baby doll's cut-off ear, get sent to the house by the glass dolphin family, Erica didn't get mad at all for my making the game too scary. Instead, she made the mother doll faint before she called the Counter-terrorist Unit for help.

It was completely perfect.

We were making the glass cats solve the crime when all of a sudden Erica's bedroom door burst open and this boy came in, going, 'What's with all the screaming in here?'

'Allie,' Erica said, all calmly, like boys burst into her room all the time, 'this is my brother, John. He's in eighth grade. John, this is Allie. Her family is moving in next door. We weren't screaming; we're just playing. These dolphins kidnapped the doll-house baby. It's a real tragedy. But it's OK, because the CTU is on the case.'

'You're moving in next door?' John looked concerned. 'Then I suppose you've heard.'

'Heard about what?' I wanted to know.

'About the reason the last family had to move out,' John said.

'No,' I said. 'We never met them. They were all moved out when we got the keys.'

'Oh,' John said. He shook his head. 'Then I probably shouldn't say anything.'

'John,' Erica said, 'what do you mean? The Ellises moved out because they retired and bought a condo in Miami.'

'Yes,' John said. 'That's what they want everyone to think. Just take my advice, Allie. Don't go in the attic.'

'The attic?' I widened my eyes, thinking about that long pull cord in the middle of the hallway on the third floor and that movie I saw where the zombie hand came out of the attic and killed those people. 'Why? What's in there?'

John made out like he was shuddering. 'Just don't go up there. OK?'

'John,' Erica said. 'What are you talking about? There's nothing –'

But then Mrs Harrington came rushing in, going on about how come I hadn't let my parents know where I was, and how they were looking all over for me and frantic with worry.

The whole time Mrs Harrington was steering me down her cream-coloured, rosebudded hallways, I kept thinking, *How had this happened? How had I gone from happily playing kidnapped dollhouse baby with my new maybe best friend to there's something evil living in the attic of my new house?*

And what could that evil thing be? What could the Ellises have left behind that was so horrible an eighth-grader – who was as tall as my dad practically – would drop his voice to a whisper when he mentioned it? As Mrs Harrington guided me down the stairs and toward the front door, I went over in my mind all the things I'd heard of that lived in people's attics.

Rats? No, that's not scary enough to bother an eighth-grader.

Bats? Gross, but again, not scary enough.

Witch? Come on. They aren't scary to eighth-graders. And they don't live in attics.

Ghost? Well, it could be a ghost. But ghosts don't

really hurt people, do they? They just pop out and scare them.

And then, just as Mrs Harrington was pushing me out the door, I remembered.

The disembodied hand. The disembodied hand had lived in the attic in that movie I had seen!

And I almost ran back inside Erica's big comfy house and begged her mom to let me come live there with them.

Because that hand had been scary! Green, glowing and so scary!

I didn't have much time to think about it though, because Mom and Dad were waiting for me in the Harringtons' front yard, and they were *really* mad at me for going next door without telling them where I was going (even though back in Walnut Knolls I can go over to Mary Kay's house without asking whenever I want. Well, pretty much).

But that apparently didn't matter. I was in Big Trouble.

I tried to tell Mom and Dad what Erica's brother had said. I tried to tell them all the way back to our house and into the car, and all the way home.

But they both looked at me blankly. Mom kept saying, 'Allie, we met the Ellises. They're lovely people.'

Dad kept saying, 'And we've been in the attic. There's nothing there except a few old boxes.'

'Have you looked *inside* them?' I asked. 'Because that's probably where it is.'

'Where what is, Allie?' Dad wanted to know.

'The thing,' I said. I didn't want to say it in front of Mark and Kevin, who were in the back seat with me, enjoying their vanilla twist cherry dip and vanilla twist butterscotch dip, respectively (my punishment for going off without telling my parents where I was going was that everyone else got ice cream at Dairy Queen on our way home. Everyone else but me).

'*You know*,' I said meaningfully to Mom and Dad. I didn't want to scare Mark and Kevin by talking about what John had said in front of them.

On the other hand, they *do* have to grow up sometime. And this was, after all, a matter of life and death.

'The thing that could come out in the night and –' I pantomimed a hand choking me to death.

'Allie,' Mom said, 'has your Uncle Jay been letting you stay up to watch horror movies with him when he babysits you kids?'

'Maybe,' I said. Like I would ever give away my secret pact with Uncle Jay. He swore he'd never rat me out about the horror movies if I swore I'd never rat him out about what really happened to Dad's scuba watch.

My mom says Uncle Jay, who is Dad's brother, suffers from Peter Pan syndrome, meaning he never wants to grow up. But Dad says he's just like all the other graduate students in his classes – slightly irresponsible.

Which is what they keep calling me for going over to Erica's house without telling them and not watching my brothers like I was supposed to.

But if you ask me, going over to Erica's was very responsible. Because if I hadn't, no one in our family would know the truth about our new house.

That's probably why Mom and Dad were able to get it so cheap. How else could they afford such a big house with so many bedrooms, even if Mom *does* have a job now and Dad has a chair? Haunted houses are cheap. Especially ones you have to fix up yourself. Everybody knows that.

'Sweetie,' Mom says. 'There's nothing in those boxes but some old junk that we're planning on throwing away as soon as we get the dumpster delivered. The next time we go to the house, I'll take you up into the attic and show you.'

'*I'm* not going up there,' I declared firmly.

'I'll go,' Mark said, cherry dip dribbling down his chin in a disgusting manner. 'I'm not afraid.'

'I'm not afraid either,' I said. 'Except for you. I just don't want to see either of you murdered in your bed by a zombie hand.'

'There are no zombie hands in the attic,' Dad said. 'I don't know what that boy next door was telling you, Allie, but he was pulling your leg.'

But they don't know. Zombie hands can't be stopped, no matter what you do to them. Even if you come after them with a chainsaw, like the guy did in that movie I watched with Uncle Jay.

But what does that matter to Mom and Dad anyway? They don't have to sleep up there on the third floor, right beneath the attic, with that trapdoor and that cord hanging down.

The truth is, we're doomed.

And they don't even know it. Or care. Mom even said, 'Allie, I don't like this kind of talk. You're scaring your little brothers –' 'No, she's not,' both Mark and Kevin said, but she ignored them – 'and if you keep up this kind of behaviour – going over to strangers' houses without telling us and spreading wild stories about zombie hands – I know one little girl who may not be getting a kitten after all.'

Moving Day

But if she thinks that's going to stop me, well, she doesn't know me at all.

And that night when we got home, after Dad got back from giving Marvin his evening walk, I sneaked out and wrestled that FOR SALE sign Mrs Klinghoffer had sunk into our yard right out of the ground. Then I hid it behind the dirt pile of the house they're building behind ours.

I know if I ever get caught, it will mean worse than having to give up dessert. It will mean I won't get my kitten for absolute sure.

But if no one else is going to try to save our family, well, I guess I'm just going to have to be the one to do it. What's a kitten (especially one that you don't even have yet) compared to keeping your whole family safe from potential evil, particularly in the form of a zombie hand?

Although I would have really liked a tiny grey-and-black-striped kitten like the glass one in Erica's dollhouse. I'd have named her Mewsette – Mewsie for short – and given her a pink collar and let her sleep next to me on my pillow every night.

If I had a kitten like that, it wouldn't matter if I looked out my window and didn't see the electrical tower blinking on and off any more every night. I'd have been able to fall asleep just fine without it, with Mewsie purring away next to me.

But what kind of pet owner would I be, bringing a kitten into a cold, dark, depressing house where she was just going to get her guts ripped out of her by the disembodied hand living in the attic? I mean, I couldn't let that happen to an innocent kitten!

Especially if the only way I was going to get a kitten anyway was if we moved.

And I knew for one hundred per cent certain that that was the *last* thing I wanted to do.

Oh, sure, I was going to miss not having Erica as a friend. It would have been totally nice having a non-crying friend.

But I couldn't let my parents sell our house and move into the new one. I just couldn't.

Because you can't let your family move into a haunted house.

That's not even just a rule.

It's a fact.

Rule #6

Whatever Brittany Hauser Says,
Just Do It If You Know What's Good for You

The only other person – besides Mary Kay, I mean –
in my class who didn't seem sad about the fact that I
was maybe (OK: probably) moving away was Scott
Stamphley. But that was no surprise.

At least Scott is consistent, seeing as how he hates
all the girls in our class equally. Also, without any
reason.

Too bad the same can't be said for Mary Kay, who
was still mad at me for the whole telling-Scott-I-was-
moving-on-her-birthday-after-I'd-sworn-I-wouldn't-
tell-anyone thing.

And that hadn't really been my fault.

Except I guess it sort of had.

But except for Mary Kay and Scott Stamphley, the
rest of Ms Myers's fourth-grade class were all being

super nice to me now that they knew that I was moving.

For instance, I now got regularly nominated to be team captain in PE. This meant I got to pick whoever I wanted for my team every day in gym class.

Not only that, but at lunch every day Mrs Fleener let me have chocolate milk even though Mom had only paid for regular for the month.

Also, Ms Myers started putting my A+ science and math papers on the board next to her desk and picking my dog drawings to hang on the wall outside the art room (not to brag, but maybe because I live with a dog on a daily basis, I am pretty good at drawing them, especially in sitting or begging-for-bones positions).

These were the good things about moving – the *only* good things about it – the things that made me not want to say to everyone, 'Um, you know what? Actually, if things go according to plan, we won't be moving after all. But thanks.'

Then there were the bad things about moving – I mean, aside from my having to leave behind my rock collection, the possible zombie hand in the attic, my horrible new room, having to start over at a new school and all that.

One of these bad things was that Brittany Hauser

and some of the other girls – concerned about my
falling-out with Mary Kay – kept trying to get us back
together by making up reasons why we should have
to sit by each other at lunch. Like, they'd go, 'Oh,
today everyone wearing blue has to sit on the right
side of the table. No, the *right* side . . .' And they'd
try to encourage me to pick Mary Kay when I was
captain in PE so she'd be on my team and stuff ('Allie,
you should pick Mary Kay. She's really good at crab
ball. No, really!').

I guess their reasoning was if we sat together or
Mary Kay was on my team or whatever, we'd have to
talk.

And if we talked, then we'd become friends again.

And then everything would be back to normal.

What these girls didn't understand was that
nothing was ever going to be normal again – not with
my moving, and definitely not between me and Mary
Kay. Things had stopped being normal between us
the day I'd poked Mary Kay in the uvula with the
spatula. That's why I'd had to start writing down
the rules in the first place.

Not that any of them but Mary Kay knew about
that. But still.

Anyway, none of the things Brittany and her
friends tried to do in order to get me and Mary Kay

back together again worked. Because every time
Mary Kay ended up next to me – by accident or on
purpose (because, truthfully, I was more than ready
to end our fight) – Mary Kay would realize what was
happening, get up and flounce away with her nose in
the air.

Or if she was on my team in PE she would just
stay as far away from me as she possibly could . . .
like, in the way, way outfield, where none of the balls
ever even come (which was just as well since Mary
Kay would usually scream and duck and run for
cover if a ball actually ever came close enough for her
to catch it anyway).

I told Brittany it was a lost cause. I told her to just
give it up. Mary Kay, as my mom once said, can hold
a grudge longer than anyone, including Grandma,
meaning Dad's mom, who still isn't speaking to Uncle
Jay because he dropped out of medical school to
study poetry instead.

And that was three years ago.

But Brittany wouldn't give up. She went, 'Allie,
you and Mary Kay can't stop being friends. You two
have been BFFs since kindergarten. That's too long
to just break up over something stupid like you
telling Scott Stamphley you're moving.'

'On her birthday,' I pointed out. 'When she asked

me not to mention it to anyone.' Breaking a promise to your best friend on her birthday is violating a major rule. I know that now. I mean, now that I've got my book of rules.

Too bad now is too late.

'Still,' Brittany said. 'You without Mary Kay is like peanut butter without jelly. It's like salt without pepper. It's like . . . like . . .'

'Me without you, Brit?' Courtney Wilcox asked hopefully.

Brittany eyed her. 'Um, yeah. Whatever. The *point*, Allie, is that we have to figure out a way to get you two talking again before you move.'

'Well,' I said. I didn't want to mention the truth – that I wasn't so sure I was going to be moving after all. My plan of keeping my house from selling seemed to be working. So far my parents hadn't mentioned that the FOR SALE sign was missing from our front yard. I knew there was more work to do – Mrs Klinghoffer had put ads in the newspaper and online, and there was supposed to be an open house this coming weekend.

But I could only handle one thing at a time.

Still, I'd learned a lesson from the Scott Stamphley thing. I wasn't telling anybody any more secrets, just in case.

'Look,' Brittany said. 'Just leave it to me, OK?'

I blinked at her. 'Leave what to you?'

'The Mary Kay thing. I have a plan.'

'You do?' I wasn't sure I liked the sound of that.

'Uh-huh,' Brittany said. 'A *brilliant* plan, if I do say so myself.'

I was really sure I didn't like the sound of that. The last time Brittany had had a brilliant plan – getting rid of a substitute teacher none of us liked when Ms Myers had been off sick with the flu – it had ended up with the substitute crying in the teachers' lounge and Mrs Grant, our principal, coming to our class and taking away our recess privileges for a week. Which may not have been a big deal to Brittany, who is no big fan of baseball or even softball.

But it was a big deal to me.

Still, I didn't say anything.

Because one of the other things I don't like about baseball (besides the whole waiting-until-it's-your-turn-at-bat thing) is people who get mad while they're playing it and argue over whether a ball was a strike or an out or whatever and waste everyone's time and keep me from being able to take my turn and hit the ball.

These people are bad enough.

But the worst – the absolute worst – are the

bat-throwers. These are people who get so mad during the game that they throw their bat.

In professional baseball, throwing a bat can get you automatically suspended.

My dad says bat throwing is very bad sportsmanship. The only thing worse, he says, is golf club throwing, because golf clubs can splinter if they break (as I found out when I was trying to open geodes with them) and put someone's eye out.

In our school, the worst bat-thrower isn't who you'd think. It's not Scott Stamphley.

It's Brittany Hauser. She once threw a bat so hard on the ground it bounced up and nearly hit the catcher in the head.

So that became a rule: *Never be catcher when Brittany Hauser is up to bat.*

It's not that Brittany's a bad person. She just has a bad temper. And when things don't go her way, she throws things.

That's why, *Whatever Brittany Hauser says, just do it* (that's another rule).

So when Brittany was saying she had a plan to get me and Mary Kay back together as friends, I didn't say anything like, 'Uh, Brittany, really, that's not necessary.'

Because it just so happened that Ms Myers's stapler was sitting nearby.

The other thing was, I knew Brittany's plan was going to fail. Because Mary Kay wasn't about to forgive me. Ever.

I knew that because I had gone up to Mary Kay in the cloakroom earlier that very day when no one was looking and said, 'Mary Kay. Look. I'm really sorry I did what I did. It was the stupidest thing I ever did. I didn't mean to hurt you. All I want is to be friends again. I've been writing down the rules of friendship and life and everything like I showed you and trying really hard to follow them. And I was just wondering . . . well, do you think you can you just forgive me now?'

But Mary Kay had turned around and flounced away. Like always.

So whatever Brittany was planning, it wasn't going to work. And just about everybody in the entire universe seemed to know it.

Except Brittany.

But she'd find out soon enough.

I just had to make sure I was out of firing range when she did.

Rule #7

First Impressions Are Very Important

The thing is, I probably should have asked Brittany if she had any tips on how to keep our house from being sold. I'm sure she'd have had a plan for that too.

It's just that it probably would have involved setting the place on fire.

And I still wanted to be able to actually *live* in my house.

So that was no good.

Instead, I had to concentrate on making up my own plan. I didn't know how I was going to do it, but somehow I had to keep our current, perfectly nice house from selling to somebody else so that Mom and Dad would have no choice but to sell the horrible new house to someone else.

I had learned enough about real estate in the past

few weeks (from having hung around listening to Mom talk on the phone to Mrs Klinghoffer) to know that we couldn't afford to own two houses at the same time . . . at least, not for very long.

So the obvious thing to do was keep our one good house from being sold. Then Mom and Dad would have no choice but to sell the new house.

I realize this might sound unfair. But you know what's *really* unfair? Buying a haunted house with a disembodied hand in the attic without even consulting your children about it.

Mrs Klinghoffer had already said that it all boiled down to what happened at the open house this coming weekend. An open house is when the people who have a house for sale open it up to the public and anyone who wants to can come traipsing through it, poking around in every single room, looking through everyone's stuff and deciding whether or not they want to live there.

Yeah! Anybody! Total strangers, looking through my stuff!

Mom said no one would be looking at my stuff. She said everyone would be looking at the house, like measuring the square footage and checking out the water heater and things like that.

But if that's true, why did she make us clean our

rooms better than we've ever cleaned them before in our lives? Why did we have to sort our toys into two piles, toys we want to keep and toys we never play with any more?

And why did she take the toys we never play with any more to the charity shop, to 'reduce clutter'?

And OK, it's true I've sort of outgrown my Polly Pocket Pollywood Rockin' Theme Park playset.

But that doesn't mean I want some other kid I've never met to have it!

At least she didn't make me throw my rocks out. Yet.

But that time is coming soon. I can tell.

'I can't even vacuum around them,' Mom said, complaining about all the paper bags sitting on the bottom of my closet. 'This is ridiculous. You can't just have ten bags of rocks sitting on the floor. You're going to have to get rid of them, Allie.'

'You said when we move,' I pointed out. 'And we haven't moved yet.'

'I've hired professional carpet cleaners,' Mom said. 'How are they going to shampoo under ten sacks of rocks? Allie, you have to move these. Can't you at least put them on a shelf or something?'

Actually, Mom asking me to put my rocks on a shelf made me think of something. Well, that and the fact that people would be poking around on the day of the open house, looking through our stuff.

So I did what Mom asked. I borrowed her stepladder from the garage and I moved each sack of rocks. Very, very carefully.

All I had to do was remember to move them again after the carpet cleaners left so they'd be in the perfect spot for the open house.

But I had plenty of things to worry about in the meantime. One of them was that Mom and Dad had scheduled an appointment at our new school – Pine Heights Elementary – for us to meet our new teachers. They were coming to pick us up in the middle of the school day. I was going to miss my favourite subject, science. I was pretty mad about that.

But mostly, I was nervous. What if I didn't like Pine Heights Elementary? What if I didn't like my new teacher? They still didn't even know for sure who my teacher was going to be, Mrs Hunter, Erica's teacher, or the other one, Mrs Danielson, so I was going to meet both of them. Apparently, there were more kids in the fourth grade in the Pine Heights area than there were in any other grade and they weren't sure which class they'd be able to fit me into.

While I was waiting for Mom and Dad to come pick me up, though, an even worse thought occurred to me. What if the fourth-graders at Pine Heights Elementary School didn't like *me*? It wasn't totally impossible. At least two fourth-graders in my current class – Scott Stamphley and my own ex-best friend – already didn't like me. It could totally happen!

This made me so nervous that I sort of started feeling like I might throw up.

'You know . . .' I said when Mom and Dad arrived to pick Mark and me up for our school visit (Kevin was already with them), 'I've been thinking it over and if Pine Heights really can't squeeze me in I'm fine with just staying in Walnut Knolls.'

'Nice try,' Dad said, totally unsympathetic to my situation. 'Get in the car.'

We drove to the new house and parked in the driveway there. 'Because,' Mom said, 'your new school is so close, you can walk there. We thought we'd show you the way.'

'Cool,' Mark said, picking up an acorn that had fallen off one of the huge trees in our front yard and throwing it at a bird, which of course had the good sense to fly away long before the acorn came anywhere close.

'Dad,' I said, because as a future vet I cannot tolerate even *potential* cruelty to animals.

'Mark,' Dad said.

'I knew that acorn wouldn't hit that bird,' Mark said.

'Let's all try to have a nice time together,' Dad said, 'and not throw anything.'

Which was very easy for Dad to say. He didn't have to worry about a bunch of fourth-graders potentially hating him.

'Have you ordered the velvet pirate wallpaper for my new room yet?' Kevin wanted to know.

'We're working on it, honey,' Mom said. 'What if it was just pirate wallpaper and not velvet?'

'I'll die,' Kevin said.

'Oh, look at that house,' Mom said, pointing at a huge house across the street. 'Look at the ginger-bread trim around the porch. Isn't that beautiful?'

It's amazing how your parents can concentrate on things like gingerbread trim when their children's lives are potentially going down the drain right before their very eyes.

Pine Heights Elementary *did* turn out to be close to the new house. *Too* close, if you ask me. Way too close to give the butterflies in my stomach a chance to go down. Only two streets away . . . and they weren't even busy streets. Like, you didn't even need to wait for a crossing guard to help you cross them. There was no chance of getting hit by a car while skateboarding without a helmet and having your brain splattered everywhere on those streets.

Because there were no cars.

But that didn't exactly make Pine Heights Elementary a very nice school. I mean, maybe it was nice if you like super-old buildings, like my mom does.

But if you actually had to go to school there and you were used to things at your old school, such as, oh, a cafeteria that was not also the gym and was not also the school auditorium . . . well, that was not something you would find at Pine Heights Elementary School, where the cafeteria tables slid up into the wall to make room for kids to play basketball when it was time for gym class, and where, later on, someone would set up a lot of folding chairs for when it was time to watch a play on the stage (over which also hung one of the basketball nets).

Also, Pine Heights Elementary School was very dark, just like our new house, having been built around the same time practically. Also, Pine Heights Elementary School smelled funny.

And even though the principal, Mrs Jenkins, was very nice and said they were doing everything they could to find a space for me in one of the fourth-grade classrooms, I didn't like her office, which had a red-headed boy in it who was there because he was in trouble for something. Who knows what? But he looked pretty scared.

Probably because Mrs Jenkins kills you if you get sent to her office, unlike the principal back at my old school, Mrs Grant, who asks you if everything is all right at home, then gives you a piece of liquorice and sends you back to class (which is pretty bad since one of my rules is *Liquorice is gross*. But that's not as bad as killing you).

I had to spend a lot of time with Mrs Jenkins because my mom ended up going with Kevin to kindergarten and Mark ended up going with my dad to the second grade. And Mrs Jenkins said, 'I'll take Allie upstairs and introduce her to Mrs Danielson and Mrs Hunter, then, if that's all right with you,' and my mom and dad said, 'That sounds great,' even though I shot them both looks saying *Don't! Don't leave me alone with her!*

But as usual, they ignored me. This happens a lot when you're the oldest. Your parents just assume you can take care of yourself.

Except when you go over to your new friend's house without telling them where you're going first, of course.

So then I had to talk to Mrs Jenkins all the way up

the long stairs (which, at my old school, we don't even have. We have RAMPS), which was pretty hard because her knees were creaking so loud they sounded like bags of potato chips being crumpled up inside her trousers, and I couldn't really hear what she was saying.

When we got to the first fourth-grade class and Mrs Jenkins said, 'This is room Two Oh Eight, Mrs Danielson's class,' I was really shocked because when she threw open the door and I peeked my head inside what I saw looked like a classroom from a television show about life on the prairie or something, not a modern-day classroom.

I mean, sure, it had big windows that looked over the playground (which had swing sets and a jungle gym and a baseball diamond – which my dad had pointed out with a wink we could use as our personal baseball diamond any time we wanted, even when school wasn't in session, since there was no fence around the grounds), and a chalkboard and everything.

And OK, the kids weren't wearing pantaloons or anything.

But they were sitting at these old-fashioned desks that had lids that lifted up in which they kept all their stuff (they didn't even have *lockers* at Pine Heights Elementary School).

And Mrs Danielson was wearing her hair in a BUN! And she had on a very boring grey trouser suit instead of something modern.

Worse, she had decorated her classroom with thought bubbles, like the kind that come out of cartoon characters' heads. Inside the thought bubbles were words about where stories come from. And the words said things like, *Stories come from ideas,* and *Ideas come from brainstorming,* and *After brainstorming comes outlining,* and *Good outlines come from good notecards*, and *Only after your notecards are in good order can you begin to write your story!*

Things like that take all the fun out of writing stories.

Things like that make me want to skateboard on High Street with no helmet on.

Mrs Danielson was teaching a lesson on photosynthesis. We'd done photosynthesis last month! How behind were the kids at Pine Heights Elementary?

And for a class that was learning about photosynthesis for the first time, the kids in Room 208 certainly looked . . . bored. Which didn't make any sense, because photosynthesis (the process by which green plants and some other organisms use sunlight to process foods from carbon dioxide and water) is super-interesting, not boring at all.

Unless it is being taught in a boring way.

When she saw me and Mrs Jenkins there in the doorway, Mrs Danielson laid down her chalk and asked, 'May I help you?'

'Oh, hello, Mrs Danielson,' Mrs Jenkins said. 'This is Allie Finkle. She might be joining your class in a few weeks.'

'Well, I don't know where she's going to sit,' Mrs Danielson said, with a laugh that I have to admit sounded kind, if a little Wicked Witch of the West-ish. 'We're a bit crowded here. But she'll be very welcome, of course.'

I wasn't sure I liked the sound of that (the not-knowing-where-I-was-going-to-sit part). I looked out at the sea of unfamiliar faces that made up Mrs Danielson's fourth-grade class. Sure, their teacher might welcome me. But what about her students? They didn't look particularly friendly to me. In fact, they looked downright mean . . . which made sense, in light of the thought bubbles.

Then I realized why they were all looking at *me*! They were waiting for me to say something!

This made the butterflies in my stomach turn into pterodactyls.

'Oh,' I said. Maybe they thought I was the one who wasn't very friendly! *First impressions are very important*, you know. That's a rule. *You can never make a second first impression* (also a rule). I saw it on TV.

I didn't know what to say. I couldn't believe it. Here it was, my one chance to make a good first impression and I was already blowing it!

'Um . . . thank you.' Great! My one chance to make a good first impression, and I said 'thank you'.

All the kids just stared at me. This wasn't helping the pterodactyls in my stomach any.

'Well,' Mrs Jenkins said, 'we'll let you get back to your lesson. Sorry for the interruption.'

'That's all right,' Mrs Danielson said, with a smile that didn't go all the way to her eyes. After that, to my relief Mrs Jenkins pulled me away.

The next room, 209, was Mrs Hunter's room. Mrs Hunter was Erica's teacher and, sure enough, when Mrs Jenkins opened the door to Mrs Hunter's classroom (which was exactly like Mrs Danielson's, only no one in it looked at all bored) and we peeked in I saw that Erica's head was one of the many that turned in my direction.

at her. I didn't really know what to say.
Wrinkle in Time *was one of my*

here behind the principal and me,
ud and old-timey sounding. Then a
The next thing I knew, students were
o the hallway.
s,' Mrs Hunter said, slipping off the
ng on. 'Class, please get your coats
our lines.'

rth-grade class scooted back their
o grab their coats from hooks on
e windows. Then they got into
front of the doorway, where they
l Mrs Hunter said, 'Well, go on.'
e classroom – all except Erica,
d asked, 'Can Allie come with

ns, who glanced at her watch,
ur parents know where you

l, grabbing my sleeve.
Erica where we were going.
nce that wherever it was, it
ire, possibly involving cut-

When she recognized me, Erica squealed and
waved.

'Hi, Allie!' she whispered, smiling.

I didn't know what to do. I wanted to make a good
impression, but I wasn't sure it was OK to wave back
in front of everyone. What if Mrs Hunter got mad?

But I didn't want Erica to think I didn't like her. I
settled for giving Erica a little wave and smiling while
I also paid attention to Mrs Hunter, who was the total
opposite of Mrs Danielson. Her hair wasn't in a bun.
It was actually cut short but very stylishly. And Mrs
Hunter wasn't in a trouser suit, either. She was wearing a very short skirt. With knee-high boots. With
high heels! She looked really, really modern and nice.

And her classroom wasn't decorated with thought
bubbles telling you that you couldn't start a story
until you had brainstormed, made an outline and
gotten your notecards ready. Her classroom was
decorated with moons, clouds and stars. And on the
stars, it said things like *Reach for the stars!* And on
the clouds, it said things like *Every cloud has a silver
lining!* And on the moons, it said things like *I like to
think the moon is there, even if I'm not looking at it. –
Albert Einstein.*

I could tell right away that this was a much better
classroom to be in than Room 208.

I could also tell that, if I *had* to be in any classroom in the world other than Ms Myers's, this was the one I wanted to be in.

'Well,' Mrs Jenkins said, 'I see that someone in this class has already made her acquaintance.' She meant, I realized, Erica. I could feel myself turning red with embarrassment. 'But for the rest of you – and you, Mrs Hunter – this is Allie Finkle, a fourth-grader who may be joining your class in a few weeks.'

'It's very nice to meet you, Allie Finkle,' Mrs Hunter said. When she smiled, she looked even prettier than Ms Myers, which I didn't know was possible. 'Are you moving to the neighbourhood?'

'Yes,' Erica cried, before I had a chance to say anything. 'She's moving in next door to me!'

Great. Why can't I ever make a normal first impression?

'Well,' Mrs Hunter said, smiling at me some more. 'That's nice. We look forward to having you join us.'

I didn't want to get anyone's hopes up though. Especially not Mrs Hunter's, seeing how nice she was being.

'Well,' I said. 'I don't know.'

Mrs Hunter looked confused. 'You don't know if you'll be joining us?'

'I did tell her,' Mrs Jenkins said, with a cough, 'that

Moving Day

And I wasn't wrong. Erica led me down the stairs and out of the building, across the gravel school yard and toward the baseball diamond where some of the kids had started up a game of kickball. At first I thought we were going to join them.

But to my surprise, Erica led us past the game and toward some bushes that grew alongside a high brick wall that separated the school grounds from the backyards of some houses next door to it.

I thought Erica would stop when we got to the bushes. But the next thing I knew, she was ducking down and crawling straight *into* them.

'Hey,' I said, putting on the brakes. 'What are you *doing*?'

'It's OK,' Erica said, looking back at me over her shoulder. 'Follow me.'

I hadn't sensed that Erica might be crazy when I was playing at her house the other day. But what did I know? I don't know that many people. My mom is always saying my Uncle Jay is crazy. But that's just because he spends all of his money on stereo equipment, instead of normal things, like dinner.

I looked around the playground. All of the other kids were running around, playing kickball or swinging on swings. None of the rest of them were crawling into bushes. The bushes were so thick, I couldn't see Erica once she was inside them. Who knew what was going on in there? Maybe she was a murderer and she was standing inside with an axe, and if I crawled in there after her she'd chop off my head (I saw that in a movie Uncle Jay and I watched once).

On the other hand, we'd had a really nice time playing with her dollhouse, and she hadn't murdered me then.

'Allie?' I heard Erica's voice float out from the bushes. 'Are you coming?'

I decided to risk it. It seemed highly doubtful Erica was a murderer. And what if there was something really cool back there and I missed it? I ducked down and crawled into the bushes after her.

When I came out the other side, I was surprised to see that the bushes only went on for a little while, and then you burst on out into all this open space and could stand up and walk around. What the bushes did was, they acted as a kind of privacy screen, so that from the playground what you couldn't see was that, really, there was all this room between the bushes and the brick wall, so you had this little private alley, practically, all to yourself, with a beautiful rooftop of golden autumn leaves over it from the trees in the yards next door as their branches drooped overhead.

Only Erica and I didn't have the alley all to ourselves, I saw to my surprise. Because there were these other two girls standing there, looking at me. It was another opportunity, I saw, for me to make a first impression. My stomach reacted again by getting all nervous.

'Hi,' said one of the girls, who was tall and skinny.

'Hi,' said the other girl, who was short and round.

'Allie,' Erica said. 'These are my friends, Caroline and Sophie. They're in Mrs Hunter's class too.'

'Hi,' I said, recognizing them now from Room 209. Caroline was the tall, skinny one. Sophie was the short, round one. 'I'm Allie Finkle.'

'We know,' Caroline said. Caroline didn't smile. She seemed very serious. 'Erica already told us all about you. She said you like ballet. Also, cats and baseball.'

'Yes,' I said, 'I do. But I see you guys play kickball here.'

'Yeah,' Sophie said. 'That's just at recess, because there was a problem with some people throwing bats. So Mrs Jenkins took them all away. Now we can only play kickball.'

'Oh,' I said. I thought this was pretty smart of Mrs

Jenkins. Also that this was a policy that ought to be implemented at my school.

'Erica also said you have a big imagination,' Caroline went on. 'That's why we said it was OK for her to bring you here. We only tell people about this place if they have a big imagination. If they don't, they can't see how magic it is.'

I looked around.

'I can see how magic it is, all right,' I said admiringly. 'I wish we had a place like this at my school. What do you guys do in here? Play like it's a fort?'

'Actually,' Erica said excitedly, 'we play like it's a castle.'

'Cool,' I said. Because it did look a lot like a castle, with the bricks and all. 'And you guys pretend to be princesses?'

'Queens,' Sophie said, looking disgusted. 'Princesses don't have any power.'

'Right,' Caroline said. She was starting to look less serious and more excited. 'We're queens. You can be one too if you want. Usually we play that an evil warlord wants to marry Sophie because she's so beautiful.'

Sophie smiled modestly at this when I looked at her. But with her curly brown hair and pink lips, she did look beautiful. So it really could be true.

MOVING DAY

'OK,' I said.

'Only she won't have him because she's pledged her heart to another,' Caroline went on. 'So we've barricaded ourselves in our castle, and the evil warlord is attacking us, and we're readying ourselves for battle.'

'Yeah,' Erica said happily. 'We're going to pour boiling oil on his forces!'

'Cool,' I said again, the butterflies in my stomach finally going away.

I was happy to have found girls who played such a neat game at recess. At Walnut Knolls Elementary, the new game Brittany Hauser was trying to get everyone to play was cheerleader (teaching anyone who would listen cheers she had learned from her big sister Becca).

We played queens until the bell rang, which happened before we even got to launch the catapult full of the heads of the warlord's army, which we had cut off with our pretend scimitars.

'Awww,' Erica said. 'I can't believe we have to go in. That was fun. Are you staying for lunch, Allie?'

'No,' I said. Because I could see my parents and Mark and Kevin standing by one of the side doors, looking around for me. 'I think I have to go.'

'Well, I hope you're going to be in our class,' Caroline said.

'Yeah,' Sophie said. 'I hope you don't get stuck in boring Danielson's class. That would stink!'

'That *would* stink,' I said, thinking of the thought bubbles. I was kind of shocked, but I was starting to find myself getting excited by the idea of going to Pine Heights.

Which was crazy! I didn't want to move! Zombie hand! Horrible dark bedroom!

'Well, it was nice to meet you guys,' I said just as Mom and Dad spotted me and started waving like crazy like they thought there was a chance I might miss them or something, which wasn't likely since they were the tallest people in the playground, outside of the teachers. 'But I better go.'

'Bye, Allie!' Sophie called as she went to join the line to go back into the school.

'Yeah, see you later, Allie,' Caroline said.

'Bye, Allie! See you on our street!' Erica called, hurrying off with her friends.

I went over to join my family instead of all the kids filing back into school. It was weird though. I didn't really want to.

'Well,' Mom said, looking pleased. 'I see you made some new friends.'

'Yes,' I said. 'They're in Erica's class with Mrs Hunter.'

'And what did you think of Mrs Hunter?' Dad wanted to know.

I started to say that I thought Mrs Hunter was the nicest, prettiest teacher in the whole world – nicer even than Ms Myers. But fortunately Mark cut me off.

'My new teacher,' he said, 'is so cool. Mr Manx? He has seven newts in a terrarium in class – well, there used to be eight, but one got eaten by the others. Anyway, he let me feed them. Newts eat anything that moves that can fit in their mouths. I fed them a cricket –'

'That is disgusting,' I burst out, glad of the distraction from how much I liked this school. 'The poor cricket!'

'It's the circle of life,' Mark said matter-of-factly. 'The newts eat the cricket and then poop him out and then the poop becomes fertilizer and then –'

'Kevin,' Mom said quickly, 'what did you think of your class?'

'Not much,' Kevin said. We had started walking home by then. Home? I mean, to the new house. 'That school isn't very fancy.'

'You only like things if they're fancy,' Mark said disgustedly.

'It may not be as new as your school in Walnut Knolls,' Dad said, 'but it's a very good school.'

'But it smells old,' Kevin complained. 'And it looks old.'

Right as Kevin said this our new house loomed into view, with its dark windows and creepy trees with their black branches scraping against the sky.

And I realized Kevin was right. He may only have been five, but he'd reminded me of something important. That just because I'd liked Mrs Hunter and Erica's friends didn't mean I wanted to move. I couldn't move. I wasn't ready to give up my old friends and my old school and my old house. Not to move into a new house that was falling down so badly they wouldn't have even let it on *Please Come Fix Up My House*. That was also, by the way, haunted. No way!

'I don't think we can get as good an education at Pine Heights as we can in Walnut Knolls,' I said.

'Allie!' Mom cried. 'Don't be ridiculous! Of course you can! How can you even say that?'

Because of the zombie hand, I wanted to say.

And I knew I had to forget about Mrs Hunter and *Reach for the stars!* And the secret castle and the game of queens. I had to forget about Erica and Caroline and Sophie. I had to harden my heart against them because the important thing was that I had to keep us from moving. Lives were at stake!

'I hated Pine Heights,' I lied. 'I hated it a lot.'

'Allie,' Mom said, sounding hurt. 'We met Mrs Hunter. She seemed really nice. I know the principal is doing everything she can to get you into her class.'

'She is?' I didn't mean to sound hopeful. 'I mean . . . I don't care.'

'And you seemed to like those girls we saw you with at recess,' Dad said.

'Yeah,' I said with a shrug. 'They were . . . OK.'

'What about your kitten?' Mom asked. 'Don't you want a kitten any more?'

That was the thing. Of course I still wanted a kitten. More than anything. Every time anyone said the word 'kitten', my heart gave a pang.

But was having a kitten worth suffering the fate of the ZOMBIE HAND?

No. No, no, no. And also, no.

And I couldn't let nice, pretty teachers and fun new girls distract me from the fact that I still had a war to win.

The war on my family moving.

Rule #8

Don't Put Your Cat in a Suitcase

On the day of the open house, Mom and Dad dropped each of us kids off at different people's homes to play so we wouldn't be in the way. They even took Marvin to stay with Uncle Jay at his apartment on campus so he wouldn't bark at all the people coming in and out of our house or get muddy paw prints on the newly shampooed carpets.

I got dropped off at Brittany Hauser's. Even though Brittany has no best friend potential because she's a bat-thrower, she's fun to play with sometimes because she has two older sisters and thus owns every Barbie and Bratz (plus all their accessories) known to humankind.

Plus, the Hausers have very excellent snack foods at their house that we aren't allowed to have at mine, including Coca-Cola of the non-diet variety and home-made brownies, because Mrs Hauser stays home all day making delicious baked goods.

On top of which, there was Brittany's mom's new cat, specifically, her show cat, meaning the kind you take around the country and get judged in contests. Only not like the county fair. Important national cat-judging contests like they have on TV.

Mrs Hauser, who is a mom who wears high heels to pick up her daughter from school, instead of jogging shoes like all the other moms, really wanted a show cat, so finally, for their anniversary, Mr Hauser bought Mrs Hauser one of her own. Mrs Hauser was very proud of it, and when she found out I might be getting a kitten – because I did my informal oral essay on it in class as soon as I knew I was getting one (but before I'd found out about the zombie hand), and Brittany heard it and told her mom – she told Brittany to invite me over to meet her registered pure-bred long-haired blue colourpoint Persian, Lady Serena Archibald.

Even though I knew I wouldn't be getting a kitten any more (especially not after what I knew was going to happen at the open house), I was very excited to meet Lady Serena Archibald. It is not every day you get to meet a registered show cat. When I had found out I might be getting a kitten I had checked out all the books on cats that were available in my school library, so I had read quite a lot on Persians and I knew that they were one of the oldest breeds of domestic longhairs.

So I couldn't wait to go to Brittany's house.

I was also a little bit excited not to be spending time with my brothers and parents. It was going to be nice to be away from my own worries about moving and the attic and to have someone my own age to talk to outside of a school setting for a change.

At least, that's what I was thinking until Mom and Dad dropped me off at Brittany's house. When I walked in the door, I stopped thinking my time hanging out with Brittany was going to be so fun.

That's because as soon as I walked in, I right away saw that the whole thing had been a set-up – at least from Brittany's side of things. In fact, it all turned out to be part of Brittany's 'brilliant plan' to make Mary Kay and me be friends again.

'Surprise!' Brittany yelled as soon as I came through the door. 'I invited Mary Kay too! Now you guys will *have* to start talking again! Because you can't be in the same house all day and not talk.'

'Wanna bet?' Mary Kay asked, glaring at me. It was obvious Brittany had not warned her beforehand either of the touching reunion she was planning for the two of us.

It was also obvious from her angry expression that Mary Kay was not backing down one inch on the whole still-being-mad-at-me thing.

'Come on, you guys,' Brittany said, taking us each by the hand and looking into our eyes very meaningfully. 'You've been best friends too long to let something as stupid as Scott Stamphley get in the way of your true bond. Mary Kay, Allie is only going to be in school with us for another few weeks. Are you really going to stay mad at her that whole time?'

'Yeah, come on, Mary Kay,' Courtney Wilcox said. Because it turned out Courtney had been invited to come along for the reunion too. Even though I had no idea what she had to do with any of it. 'Allie didn't mean anything by it. Did you, Allie?'

I sighed. I could see all my fun plans for playing with Lady Serena Archibald – not to mention Brittany's huge Barbie and Bratz collections, all of which, by the way, still have their shoes and feet – vanishing into thin air.

I thought about asking to use the phone and calling my mom and having her come pick me up. Only two things kept me from doing so. One was what I knew was about to happen at the open house with my rock collection.

The other was the fact that Brittany was standing kind of close to a life-size ceramic figurine of a cat (in addition to having a real show cat, Mrs Hauser collects ceramic figurines of them as well), and I was afraid if I tried to leave, thwarting her brilliant plan to get us back together, Brittany might throw it at me.

'No,' I said. 'Of course I didn't mean it.'

Mary Kay glared at the floor. The tops of her ears were turning red, a sure sign she was getting ready to cry.

Only not because she was sad. Because she was angry.

'Allie *promised*,' Mary Kay said. Only not to me. She was apparently speaking to the floor, because that's what she was looking at. 'She promised not to tell anyone she was moving because it was *my* special day, and I asked her not to. And then what did she do? She turned around, and she told. *Scott Stamphley*, of all people. That's who she told. After she PROMISED.'

'I know I promised,' I said. I seriously felt terrible. Like I hadn't been feeling terrible about my broken promise – on top of a lot of other things – for weeks now. 'But I temporarily forgot. Are you really going to hold temporarily forgetting for one minute against me for the rest of my life? I mean, you've temporarily forgotten stuff.'

Mary Kay lifted her gaze and fastened it on me. 'Like what?'

To be honest, I couldn't exactly remember anything at that particular moment that Mary Kay had temporarily forgotten. I was totally sure there'd been some stuff. I just couldn't think what.

'I don't know,' I admitted. 'But, like . . . stuff.'

'This is ridiculous,' Mary Kay said with a sniff. 'I'm not staying here. I want to go home. I'm calling my mother.'

And she made a move to head toward Brittany's kitchen where the nearest phone was.

Brittany was too fast for her though. She stepped right into Mary Kay's path.

And sure enough, I saw her hand come to rest on the nearby cat figurine.

What's more, Mary Kay saw it too. And she grew very still.

Everyone knows about Brittany's reputation as a bat-thrower. *Everyone.*

'Nobody's going home,' Brittany said in a hard voice. 'Everybody is staying right here. I have some nice games planned, and some nice snacks for us to eat. And we're going to play them, and eat them, and have a good time. Does everyone understand?'

Mary Kay looked a little scared. I didn't really blame her. Brittany scared me a little too.

But for once Mary Kay didn't start crying.

Instead, she said, 'OK, Brittany,' in this voice I'd never heard her use before, but which sounded kind of familiar.

Then a second later, I heard Courtney go, 'Oh, there's Lady Serena Archibald!'

'Keep her away from me!' Mary Kay squealed. 'You know I'm allergic!' That's when I realized the reason why the voice Mary Kay was using sounded familiar to me. That's because it was almost exactly like Courtney's voice, which was actually almost exactly like Brittany's voice. Because Courtney is always trying to imitate Brittany.

Then I realized Mary Kay was trying to imitate Brittany too.

Which was kind of weird.

But I didn't think about it then because I was too excited about seeing Lady Serena Archibald, a real-life show cat.

And to tell you the truth, the wait was totally worth it. Lady Serena Archibald was beautiful. She had long, silky grey fur and big blue eyes. And when

Moving Day

I went over to pet her, Lady Serena Archibald turned those big blue eyes up to look at me and she opened her tiny mouth and went, 'Mrow?' in the cutest way you could ever possibly imagine.

Mrs Hauser followed her cat into the room, her high heels click-clacking on the marble floor of the Hausers' entranceway, and said, smiling, 'Oh, Allie, I'm so glad you could come. You're finally getting to meet Lady Serena. What do you think? Don't you think you'd like a Persian now?'

Then Mrs Hauser went on to tell me about the care of Persian show cats – like how you have to brush their fur every day because it's so long they can't clean it with their tongue like cats normally do, and how Lady Serena Archibald had never been outside, and so how we had to be careful not to let her out of the house – even though I already knew most of it from the books I read.

But I pretended like I didn't know already – and that there was still a chance I was going to get a kitten when, in fact, after today there was absolutely no way – and listened quietly because that's the polite thing to do when an adult is telling you something you already know, especially when they're doing it all excitedly like Mrs Hauser was doing.

That's a rule, by the way.

When Mrs Hauser was finally done talking and said she had to go drive Brittany's older sister Bethany to her band rehearsal – adding that we shouldn't bother Brittany's other older sister, Becca, who was in the garage with her friends painting posters for their school's bake sale on Monday – Brittany muttered, 'I thought she'd never leave,' and Courtney laughed. Even Mary Kay tittered a little.

But truthfully I'd thought what Mrs Hauser had been saying was interesting, even if I'd already known about most of it on account of the books I'd read and my wanting to be a vet when I grow up and all.

'Now that she's gone,' Brittany said, 'we can go to my room and get down to business.'

I wasn't sure I liked the sound of that.

'What kind of business?' I wanted to know, hoping it was going to involve Bratz, or at least Barbie.

'The business of getting you and Mary Kay back together as friends,' Brittany replied. 'Now, let go of that cat and come on.'

I let go of Lady Serena even though I didn't really want to and followed Brittany up to her room, where there was absolutely no discussion about what we were going to do next. Brittany didn't go, 'So, do you guys want to play a game? How about queens?' or 'Do you want to get out my sisters' Barbies?' She didn't even go, 'I know! Do you want to play lions?'

Instead, she went, 'OK, we're playing pop star. I'm the judge.'

She didn't even explain how you play pop star, which, by the way, I had never heard of. We're not allowed to watch reality shows or even music videos in my house because my mother says they rot your brain. Instead, she makes us watch Quality Pro-grammes, even though I've explained to her that this puts me at a disadvantage in most social situations.

'Whoever does the best job,' Brittany went on, 'wins a brownie. There's the microphone. Courtney, you go first.'

And Courtney picked up this microphone that was lying on Brittany's super-frilly pink canopy bed, turned on a mini-karaoke machine that was sitting in the middle of Brittany's super-pink frilly room (which was even pinker and frillier than my room), and started singing along with this CD that was play-ing.

When she was done, Mary Kay clapped and went, 'Oh, my gosh, Courtney, that was so good!' So I said, 'Um, yeah, it was,' although truthfully I didn't like the dance Courtney had been doing along with the song. It was kind of boring. It didn't have any jumps in it. Actually, the song had been boring too, just the words 'baby, baby' over and over again.

Frankly, I wished I was back behind the bushes by Pine Heights playing queens with Erica, Caroline and Sophie. That had been much more fun.

But I didn't say so out loud because that wouldn't have been polite. That's a rule.

'OK, Mary Kay,' Brittany said. She had taken up her judging position in the midst of all the pillows in the middle of her bed. 'Your turn.'

Mary Kay looked all shocked. 'Oh, no!' she said. 'I couldn't! I'll never do as good a job as Courtney.'

'What are you talking about, Mary Kay?' I asked. 'You sing songs like that all the time to the mirror in your bathroom.'

Mary Kay shot me a mean look.

'Well,' I said, 'you do. And you do dances to them too.' How was I supposed to know that was a secret? Mary Kay had never said so.

This is why I need the rules. Friendship is so COMPLICATED.

Mary Kay got up from where she was sitting on one of Brittany's white beanbag chairs and took the microphone from Courtney. Then she turned on the CD and did the same song Courtney had done. And basically the same dance along with it. Only

Moving Day

Mary Kay's dance was even more boring than Court-ney's had been. Except it was obvious Mary Kay had been practising this dance a LOT in the full-length mirror on the back of her closet door, because she put a lot of hip wiggles into it.

When she was done all three of us applauded, even though I thought I was going to die of boredom the whole time. At that point, I'd rather have been playing lions. I'd even have been the boy lion. I'd have gladly gotten rug burns going out and killing an antelope and bringing it home for all the mother lions and baby cubs to eat. That's how bored I was.

'OK, Allie,' Brittany said. 'Your turn.'

I knew I was in trouble. I didn't know the song, although I could see that the words came up on the karaoke machine's screen, and I didn't know the dance either. There was no way I was going to win.

Which stank because I was really getting hungry. I could definitely have used one of Mrs Hauser's deli-cious home-baked brownies. It wasn't fair of Brittany only to give out brownies as prizes. Really, everyone should get a brownie, no matter how well or not they sang. That was the polite way to treat your guests, after all.

Oh, well. Maybe when Mrs Hauser got back from dropping off Bethany she'd give us all lunch. She was going to have to, right? I mean, you can't let your guests starve. That's a rule. I'm almost sure.

'Come on,' Brittany said from her pillow throne. 'We don't have all day, Allie.'

I was surprised to realize I was kind of nervous. Which was weird, because Brittany and Courtney and Mary Kay were my friends. Well, except for Mary Kay, who was my ex-friend. My ex-best friend.

Still, why should I be nervous about singing in front of them? It's true I'm not the best singer, but I'm not the worst either.

It's just . . . I didn't want to look dumb all of a sudden. It wasn't even about the brownie any more. I just didn't want them to laugh at me.

'Come *on*,' Brittany said.

Realizing I had no choice but to get on with it, I switched on the CD. The words of the song came on. Boy, that was fast. It didn't even give me time to warm up. Suddenly, I had to start singing.

'LOUDER,' Brittany yelled.

I tried to sing louder.

'You have to dance too,' Brittany yelled.

The problem was, I couldn't read the words and dance at the same time. I mean, if I was dancing, I couldn't see the words on the screen.

But as I stood there, I realized the words weren't

that hard. They really were the same words – 'baby, baby' – over and over. And also, I had just heard the song twice already. So it turned out I kind of did know the words.

That's when I got an idea. And my idea was to do a different dance than the one Courtney and Mary Kay had done. My idea was to do some ballet. To make the dance more interesting.

So I started doing some pliés and relevés and stuff.

'WHAT ARE YOU DOING?' Brittany demanded. I heard Courtney and Mary Kay laughing.

But I didn't care. I was having fun. Ballet turned out to go kind of good with the song.

But it really needed something else. What it needed, I realized, were some jumps. So I started throwing in some grand jetés. It was kind of hard to do them and still hold the microphone – not to mention sing – but I managed. I started doing grand jetés all around Brittany's room. They were good ones too. If Madame Linda had been there, I'm sure she'd have let me wear her tiara during cooldown.

'STOP IT,' Brittany said. 'THAT IS NOT PART OF THE SONG!'

But it was too late. The song was over, and so were my grand jetés. I did a curtsy – the ballet kind, which is called a reverence and is super low.

Courtney and Mary Kay applauded.

'Stop clapping,' Brittany told them. And they did, looking guilty.

'What,' Brittany demanded, glaring at me, 'was *that*?'

'Ballet,' I said.

'Well,' Brittany said. 'You do *not* win the brownie.' She looked at Mary Kay. '*You* do.'

'Oh,' Mary Kay said. 'Thanks.'

'Go down to the kitchen and get one,' Brittany said. 'They're sitting on a plate on the counter.'

'OK,' Mary Kay said. She got off the bed and left the room.

'Now,' Brittany said, when she was gone. 'What are we going to do to make her start speaking to you again, Allie?'

'Well,' I said, feeling mad at Brittany – but I was careful not to let it show too much in case there was a baseball bat hidden inside those pillows Brittany was sitting on. 'SHE liked my dance. She was laughing.'

'She was laughing AT you,' Brittany pointed out. 'Not WITH you. No. We need to come up with something more. Something better than pop star.'

'We could have lunch,' I suggested.

'It's not time for lunch yet,' Brittany said.

Moving Day

'Yeah,' I said. 'But, I mean, when it IS time for lunch. We could all make it together. Like grilled cheese or something.'

'That's a good idea,' Brittany said, and I felt myself flush with pride because I had actually said something Brittany approved of. 'Only not grilled cheese. Mini pizzas.'

This didn't sound so good to me. Because the problem with pizza is, it violates one of my rules, which is never eat anything red.

'This would be OK,' I said hesitantly. 'As long as we didn't have to put tomato sauce on them.'

'Don't be stupid,' Brittany said. 'Of course you have to put tomato sauce on them. They're *pizzas*.'

'Actually,' I said. 'There's something called white pizza, and that's just –'

'YOU HAVE TO HAVE TOMATO SAUCE ON PIZZA,' Brittany screamed.

'You don't have to scream, Brittany,' I said. 'I'm standing right here; I can hear you just fine.'

'I guess I do have to scream,' Brittany said, 'since no one seems to be *listening* to me. Let me ask the question again. What are we going to do to get you and Mary Kay to be friends again that does not involve pizza without tomato sauce?'

I thought about it.

'We could play queens,' I suggested.

'What's *that*?' Brittany demanded.

'Oh,' I said, relieved she'd asked. 'It's a really fun game. We can pretend your room is a castle, OK? And there's an evil warlord who's in love with one of us. And his forces are storming the castle, and we have to protect it by pouring boiling oil on them.'

'Who do I get to be?' Courtney wanted to know.

'You can be the queen he's in love with,' I said. 'Or one of the other queens.'

'I AM NOT GOING TO PLAY SOME STUPID GAME ABOUT PRETEND QUEENS,' Brittany screamed.

'Hey.' Mary Kay appeared in the doorway. She was holding the most delicious-looking brownie I had ever seen. 'Oh, no! Look who followed me upstairs!'

She looked down, and we all followed her gaze. And there, rubbing the door frame with her big, squished Persian head, was Lady Serena Archibald.

'She's making my eyes water,' Mary Kay wailed.

'Awww,' I said. I went over to start petting Lady Serena. Lady Serena was one of those cats who liked being petted. She pushed her head into my hand and purred, hard.

'Oh!' Brittany cried, leaping off the bed all of a

sudden. 'I know a really fun game! Much better than *your* stupid game, Allie.'

Courtney leaped off the bed too. 'I know what game you mean!' she cried. 'If it's the one I'm thinking of.'

'It is,' Brittany said. 'It's called lady business executive. It's super hilarious.'

Courtney was already laughing. 'Oh, my gosh, I laughed so hard the last time we played I almost wet my pants!'

'This brownie is so good,' Mary Kay said, with her mouth full. 'Too bad everyone can't have one.'

'Yeah, too bad,' Brittany said. She was barely listening. She was too busy rooting through her closet for something.

I flashed Mary Kay a mean look as I petted Lady Serena. She just smiled as she chewed her brownie, her 'allergies' temporarily forgotten.

Seriously, I can't believe we were ever even friends.

Courtney, watching Mary Kay chew, said faintly, 'Gosh. I sure am hungry.'

'Here it is!' Brittany cried triumphantly. And she pulled, from the depths of her closet, a big, hard plastic suitcase . . . the kind with wheels on the bottom that you can pull through airports.

'What do you have that for?' I asked. Every time I

stopped petting Lady Serena she would bump my hand with her head to get me to start petting her some more. She was so cute. It almost broke my heart I was never going to have one. A cat of my own, I mean.

But the funny thing was, when Lady Serena Archibald saw that suitcase, she stopped butting her head against me and suddenly bolted for the door.

'Shut the door!' Brittany yelled. 'Don't let her get away!'

Mary Kay, who was still in the doorway enjoying the last of her brownie, slammed the door shut just as Lady Serena Archibald came streaking toward it, cutting off her only means of escape.

'Grab her!' Brittany yelled, and Mary Kay stooped down and caught Lady Serena up in her still chocolatey hands, her allergies completely forgotten now.

Lady Serena didn't like this and let out a yowl.

I have to admit I didn't like this very much either.

'Hey,' I said. 'What are you guys going to do?'

'I told you,' Brittany said. 'We're playing lady business executive. Now, put Lady Serena in the suitcase.'

'WHAT?' I couldn't believe what I was hearing.

'Go on,' Brittany said to Mary Kay, who'd hesitated. 'It's OK. Lady Serena likes it.'

But I could tell, from the way Lady Serena

Moving Day

Archibald was arching her back and trying to sink her claws and teeth into Mary Kay as she bent to put the cat into the suitcase, that she didn't like it. She didn't like it at all.

'You guys,' I said, feeling a little sick all of a sudden. 'I don't think this is a very good idea.'

'No,' Brittany said as she snapped the lid of the suitcase closed, trapping Lady Serena Archibald inside. 'It's fine. Courtney and I play this all the time. It's really fun.'

'But she can't *breathe* in there,' I said.

'Of course she can,' Brittany said. 'Listen.'

We were all quiet for a minute. Then, from inside the suitcase, we heard a ghostly wail. It was Lady Serena Archibald, letting us know how unhappy she was.

'See?' Brittany said. 'If she couldn't breathe, how could she make that sound?'

'That sound,' I pointed out, 'means she doesn't like it. You should let her out. Or –' I added this next part in desperation, since Brittany wasn't listening to me – 'your mom is going to be mad.'

'Only if she finds out,' Brittany said with a shrug. 'Now, come on. I'll be the lady business executive. I have a very important flight to catch.' Brittany jerked up the suitcase's handle and began to drag the suitcase around the room by its wheels. As she did so Lady Serena Archibald's wailing increased in volume.

Courtney started to giggle.

'It sounds so funny!' she cried. 'Like a baby.'

It did sound like a baby. Like a really unhappy baby.

'I have to hurry,' Brittany said, looking at an imaginary watch on her wrist. 'I'm going to miss my flight.'

She started walking faster. Lady Serena Archibald began to meow. But not just any meow. Very loud meows. That sounded, incidentally, exactly like the word 'meow'. *Meow. Meow.* Then, as Brittany whipped the suitcase around even faster, more loudly – *MEOW! MEOW!*

'Oh, no,' Mary Kay said, collapsing in giggles on to the bed. 'She did not just say that. Tell me she didn't just say "meow" like that!'

Brittany suddenly jerked the suitcase to a halt, causing Lady Serena Archibald, inside of it, to slide around with a thump.

'What do you MEAN, my flight has been cancelled?' Brittany demanded, looking horrified.

From inside the suitcase, Lady Serena Archibald let out a long, low growl.

Moving Day

'Is that a cat in there?' Courtney wanted to know, gasping because she was laughing so hard. 'Or a bear?'

'Uh-oh,' Brittany said, lifting up the suitcase and beginning to swing it back and forth, causing Lady Serena Archibald to slide with a thump from side to side inside. 'Time for the baggage carousel –'

'NO!' I yelled.

And before I knew what I was doing, I had ripped the suitcase out of Brittany's hands.

'Allie!' Brittany yelled. 'What are you –'

But I had already put the suitcase on the floor and was undoing the latches.

'No, don't!' Brittany yelled.

But it was too late. I threw open the lid, and a split second later, Lady Serena Archibald came whipping out, all of her fur standing on end, her blue eyes whirling crazily.

'Catch her!' Brittany yelled. 'Don't let her get away!'

Courtney and Mary Kay dived for the cat. But I was determined not to let Mrs Hauser's show cat be abused any more that day. I went over to Brittany's bedroom door.

'Don't you open that door, Allie Finkle,' Brittany yelled. 'Not if you know what's good for you!'

I opened the door.

Lady Serena Archibald shot through, nothing but a soft grey blur and crazy pinwheel eyes as she made a frantic break for freedom.

'After her!' Brittany shrieked.

I couldn't believe it. I couldn't believe Brittany was being so mean to her mom's cat.

'You guys,' I said. 'Come on. Let's just play something else. How about Barbies?'

'Barbies are for babies,' Brittany hurled at me as she tore past me and down the hall, chasing after poor Lady Serena Archibald, who had made it down the stairs and into the entranceway.

I had no choice but to follow the other girls. I had to make sure they didn't catch the poor cat and put her back in that suitcase.

'She's in the den,' I heard Brittany yelling from somewhere in the Hausers' enormous house.

'I thought I saw her go into the living room,' Courtney yelled back.

'I think she went into the laundry room,' Mary Kay cried.

But they were all wrong. Because I found Lady Serena Archibald trembling beside a closed door off the kitchen, looking up at me with her big, sad eyes, begging me to open the door and allow her to escape.

MOVING DAY

And so I did . . .

Just as Brittany came rushing in.

'Allie, no!' she shouted.

But it was too late. Lady Serena, hearing the voice of her mortal enemy, streaked through that door and to freedom.

'You IDIOT!' Brittany yelled at me.

'Too bad,' I said, closing the door behind Lady Serena Archibald. Suddenly, I didn't care that Brittany was standing really close to another one of her mother's ceramic cat figurines. Let her throw it at me. So what if I had to get stitches? Maybe then I'd get to go home. 'But you know, Brittany, cruelty to animals is a serious crime. You can go to jail for it. Besides, Lady Serena will be fine in the basement.'

'That isn't the basement door, stupid,' Brittany raged. 'That's the door to the garage, and my sister is out there making her posters with the *garage door open*! You just let Lady Serena Archibald out, and she's NEVER BEEN OUTSIDE BEFORE!'

Rule #9

When You Do Something Wrong, Always Apologize
(Even If It's Not Entirely Your Fault)

We spent the whole rest of the afternoon looking for Lady Serena Archibald in the Hausers' neighbourhood.

Unfortunately, she was nowhere to be found.

I thought maybe she'd still be hiding in the garage. Neither Becca nor any of Becca's friends had actually seen her leave the garage.

And there were lots of ski boots and coolers and old models of volcanoes (ancient science projects of Brittany's sisters) out there on shelves that she could have been hiding behind.

But we looked in and around and even under all that stuff, and she wasn't there.

There was really only one conclusion to be drawn. And that's that she had gotten out.

Lady Serena Archibald, champion Persian show

cat, was wandering around in the wilds of Walnut Knolls. Who even knew if she'd ever come home? I mean, after the way Brittany had treated her, if I'd been her, I wouldn't have.

But of course, when Mrs Hauser got back from her errands (with pizza and cheesy breadsticks for us for lunch, because my mom had warned her about how I wouldn't eat anything red), we couldn't tell that part to her. I mean, the part about *why* I'd let her cat out. I just said that I'd made a mistake. I said that Lady Serena Archibald had been sitting by the door meowing (which was not even a lie), and I thought it was the door to where they kept her litter box or something and so I'd opened it and let her out without looking.

The whole thing, I'd told Mrs Hauser without being able to look her in the eye, was my fault.

And that I was really, really sorry.

Mrs Hauser was nice about it. She was more worried about Lady Serena Archibald than anything else. She called the police and everything (even though I guess they sort of laughed at her because she hung up very fast afterward and said, 'Well, Lady Serena may be just a cat to them, but she's like a child to ME!').

She also called animal control and the neighbourhood association to ask them to keep an eye out for any stray long-haired blue colourpoint Persian cats who might be roaming around.

Then we all put our jackets on and started walking around the yard, calling, 'Here, Lady Serena Archibald. Here, kitty, kitty,' and shaking bags of Lady Serena's favourite dry food and tapping spoons on cans of her favourite wet food.

None of it worked though. Lady Serena Archibald didn't come home. The people at animal control said most likely she would when she was ready, even when Mrs Hauser explained that Lady Serena had never been outside before and probably didn't even know how to GET home.

Even though Mrs Hauser was nice about my letting her cat out, her youngest daughter sure wasn't. Every chance she got, Brittany leaned over and hissed, 'I'll get you for this.' Which I didn't think was very nice, because it really wasn't my fault. I mean, it was, but it wasn't.

'I didn't tell,' I said to her, meaning about the suitcase.

'It doesn't matter,' Brittany whispered back. 'I did this all for you anyway. You're the one who's moving. I wanted to make your last weeks here special by making Mary Kay like you again. But now I see why she doesn't. You ruin everything, Allie Finkle.'

Moving Day

This was kind of hard to hear. Especially since I knew it wasn't true. The truth was, Brittany Hauser was the ruiner. Especially the ruiner of cats.

At that moment, I was kind of glad I might be moving. I was kind of glad I might be going away and never going to see any of these people again.

By the time Mom came to pick me up, the only person who was speaking to me was Mrs Hauser.

'Don't worry, Allie,' she said as I climbed into our car. 'I'm sure Lady Serena Archibald will come home when she gets hungry.'

It was kind of hard to believe she really even thought this though. Because I could see the tears in her eyes. She was just trying to be brave. She loved that cat *so much*, even though she'd only had her a few months.

The thing was, I could totally see why. If I had let my parents move and give me Mewsette, I know I'd have loved her just as much.

'I really hope so,' I said as I buckled up. 'I'm so sorry.'

'I know you are, sweetie,' Mrs Hauser said with a smile. But I could tell that beneath the smile she was as worried as I was. More worried, even.

I really didn't want to make Mrs Hauser more worried.

But I wanted to make her understand what had happened – why I had done what I had done.

And I also wanted to make sure that if Lady Serena Archibald *did* come back some day, she wouldn't need to be rescued again.

So I said, even though saying it made my stomach hurt (and not just because I hadn't been able to touch my cheesy bread, on account of not being hungry at all after losing Mrs Hauser's cat), 'It's just, I really don't think Lady Serena likes it when Brittany plays lady business executive and puts her in that suitcase.'

Mrs Hauser looked at me funny, and asked, 'What suitcase, honey?'

So I told Mrs Hauser all about lady business executive. Since Brittany was already mad at me – and I was out of missile range – I didn't think it would make any difference now.

And it might keep Lady Serena Archibald safe in the future.

Mrs Hauser got very quiet when she heard about the game her daughter secretly liked to play with her cat.

And when she learned that was the reason I'd accidentally let Lady Serena outside, she said, in a strange voice, 'I understand now. Well. Thank you,

Allie. Thank you very much for being honest with me.'

Then she turned away and yelled, '*BRITTANY!*' in the scariest voice I have ever heard.

I was glad when my mom got into the car and started it and pulled away.

'What was *that* all about?' she wanted to know.

'Brittany Hauser likes to put her mom's cat in a suitcase and shake her around,' I said. 'And I just told on her.'

My mom started to laugh, but then stopped herself.

'Well,' she said. 'You're just having a banner day, aren't you?'

'What's that supposed to mean?' I wanted to know. I was having to lean against the closed car window because my head was feeling so heavy all of a sudden. I was glad I was the first one being picked up. I don't know if I could have handled it if Mark and Kevin had been in the back seat, talking about trucks and bugs and sports and velvet wallpaper.

'I mean, not only did you lose Mrs Hauser's cat,' Mom went on, 'but maybe you'd also like to explain that little trick you did with your rock collection back home.'

I perked up at hearing the words 'trick' and 'rock collection'.

'Why?' I asked. 'Did it work?'

'If you mean did your entire rock collection spill down from the top shelf of your closet on to your bedroom floor when Nancy Klinghoffer opened the door today at the open house, then yes, it did work,' Mom said.

Yes! My trick worked! I couldn't believe it! I had planned it so long ago! And it had worked perfectly! We weren't moving! *We weren't moving!*

'I hope Mrs Klinghoffer wasn't injured,' I said, trying to hide my delight.

'No,' Mom said. 'But she could have been. And we'll have to get the carpet in your room cleaned all over again. It's completely covered in dirt and little pieces of rock.'

'Geodes,' I corrected her. 'They aren't rocks. They're geodes.'

'Honestly, Allie,' Mom said, 'I don't know what you were trying to accomplish.'

'You said to get my collection up off the floor,' I pointed out innocently. 'So I put them on the top shelf. Gosh, it's too bad they spilled. I guess we won't be able to move now, since no one will want to buy a house with such a dirty carpet.'

Moving Day

'On the contrary,' Mom said, smiling. 'We've had an offer already, and Mrs Klinghoffer's expecting two more. There's a housing shortage in this area, you know – which is why they're constantly building around here – and people are dying to move into Walnut Knolls.'

Suddenly, my stomach started hurting all over again. I couldn't believe it! My plan! My beautiful plan for keeping us from moving! It had failed! We were going to have to move into the horrible house with the zombie hand in the attic after all!

Why did people want to move to Walnut Knolls anyway? They were just going to have to send their kids to school with people like Brittany Hauser. Didn't they know what kind of damage that could do to a child?

I guess my mom could tell I felt that way, since she said, 'Allie, I know you didn't like Pine Heights Elementary very much – or at least, that's what you said. And I know you're not a big fan of the house. But I promise you'll get used to both of them. Who knows? You may even grow to like them. You haven't really given either of them a chance. I know it doesn't look like much now, but let Daddy and me work on the house. I promise you, it's not going to look the way it does now forever. Your room, for instance, is going to be lovely. When you see the window seat Daddy is building for you –'

'It's not that,' I said. 'It's –'

'We're doing the very best we can to get you into Mrs Hunter's class. I know how much you like her.'

'It's not that either,' I said.

'Well, it had better not be the zombie-hand thing,' Mom said in a different voice. 'Because you are way too old to be believing in ridiculous things like that.'

Zombie hands are not ridiculous! What's more, the first people the zombie hand kills are always the ones who don't believe in zombie hands!

'But, Mom,' I said. 'You can't *see* the zombie hand. Not until it wants you to see it. And by then it's too late.'

'I'm going to murder your Uncle Jay,' Mom said. 'And I'm not going to need zombie hands to do it either. Allie, there is nothing wrong with the attic of that house. Do you hear me? The next time we're there, I'll show you. And I don't want any more silly stunts like the one you pulled today with the rocks. Understand? Mrs Klinghoffer nearly strained her back picking up all those geodes. I don't need her chiropractic bills to pay on top of everything else.'

Hearing that Mrs Klinghoffer had had to pick up all my rocks cheered me up. But only a little. Because the truth was, Lady Serena Archibald was still missing.

And we still had to move.

But the thought of all those geodes spilling down when Mrs Klinghoffer opened my closet door did make me laugh. A little.

Even though I knew I was going to have to apologize later.

Because, of course, that's a rule.

Rule #10

**If You Get a New Best Friend,
It's Rude to Show Off About It**

Lady Serena Archibald came back Monday morning.

I didn't find that out because Brittany told me though. I found out because Courtney Wilcox told me.

And the only reason Courtney told me was because she carpools to school with Brittany and she saw the whole thing.

But Brittany told her not to tell me. Except that Courtney was mad at Brittany for telling her that she wasn't her best friend any more. Mary Kay is Brittany's new best friend. Courtney is now Brittany's second-best best friend.

I guess the whole brownie thing should have been a sign that this was coming, but none of us recognized it then for what it was.

'The truth is,' Courtney said, 'the only reason

Moving Day

Brittany gave that brownie to Mary Kay was because she was planning all along on making Mary Kay her new best friend. Your dance was really the best. Even if your singing wasn't all that good.'

I said thank you even though I wasn't sure what Courtney had said was a compliment. Because that is the polite thing to do when someone compliments you. Even if you aren't sure it's a compliment.

That's a rule.

Of course, neither Brittany nor Mary Kay was speaking to me – Brittany because I had told her mother about the suitcase game and Mrs Hauser had taken away Brittany's karaoke machine and her television privileges as well, and Mary Kay because . . . well, because I had told Scott Stamphley I was moving on her birthday when I had promised I wouldn't.

'And Lady Serena Archibald is all right?' I asked Courtney.

'Oh, yes,' Courtney said. 'I mean, her fur is all matted and dirty, because she'd been in a field and gotten into some burrs. But she was sitting on the front porch this morning when Mr Hauser went out to get the newspaper, and she was just fine – really hungry, but fine. Mrs Hauser is taking her to a professional groomer to get the burrs out and says she should be good as new.'

I was super relieved to hear that. I didn't even care about the other thing – I mean about Brittany and Mary Kay not speaking to me. The truth was, after what happened at the Hausers', I didn't want to be friends with them any more, anyway.

'I'll be your best friend, if you want, Allie,' Courtney said. 'Until you move, anyway.'

'Um,' I said. 'OK.' Because it's rude to say no to someone who asks if you want to be best friends.

What's even more rude is to do what Mary Kay and Brittany did later that day, which was come up to me in the art room, where I was innocently gouging an outline of Marvin begging for a bone into my linoleum tile, and go, 'What smells?'

'Hmmm,' Brittany said. 'I think it's Allie. Allie Stinkle smells . . . like a rat!'

I have to admit, that really hurt my feelings. But I wasn't going to cry or anything. At least, not in front of them. Because crying when people are trying to insult you just gives them what they want. Then they win, because they know they made you sad. So you have to pretend like you don't care. Then you win.

That's a rule.

Instead, I kept working on my art project and said

very calmly, like what they'd said hadn't bothered me at all, 'Wow. That's very mature, you guys.'

'Oh, right,' Brittany said. 'Like *you're* so mature! I can't believe you told my mother about lady business executive!'

'I can't believe you put an innocent cat in a suitcase,' I shot back.

'I can't believe you keep a book of *rules*,' Brittany said.

I was so shocked that she said that, I forgot about pretending not to care. In fact, I nearly jammed my lino-cutter into my thumb.

'*What* did you say?' I asked.

'That's right,' Brittany said with a smile I can only call mean. 'I know all about how you're such a weirdo you have to write down rules to remind yourself how to act, Allie. That's really pathetic. You know, I almost feel sorry for you.'

I turned my hurt gaze toward Mary Kay, who was standing next to Brittany. At least Mary Kay looked kind of uncomfortable . . . if the way she was staring at her shoes was any indication, I mean.

'You *told* her?' I croaked. 'About my book of rules?'

Mary Kay rubbed her nose with her shoulder, avoiding looking at me. Before she had a chance to say anything, Brittany went, 'Of *course* she told me about your stupid book of rules. *Never eat anything red*? Please. Who do you think you are anyway, the food police? You know what rule I think you need to add to your little book, Allie Stinkle? The rule of not being a rat. I'm so glad you're moving, so you won't continue to stink up our class with your hideous rat odour! Aren't you glad she's moving, Mary Kay?'

'Oh, yes,' Mary Kay said, perking up suddenly. 'I'm really glad *you're* my best friend now, Brittany.'

'Me too,' Brittany said, throwing an arm around Mary Kay's neck.

It was at this moment that I realized that other people were listening to our conversation and finding it very interesting. By 'other people', I mean other people at the table I was sitting at, people who were still only at the cutting stage of their block-printing project.

One of them, unfortunately, was Scott Stamphley.

'You keep a book of rules?' he asked me.

'Shut up,' I said to him. Because I might have to put up with Brittany and Mary Kay. But I do not have to put up with him.

'Are there any rules in there about me?' Scott wanted to know.

Moving Day

'Yeah,' I said. 'To stay as far away as possible from you.'

'How about this?' Scott asked. 'Is there a rule about this?'

Then he burped very loudly.

'EW!' shrieked Brittany and Mary Kay . . . which is of course exactly the kind of reaction boys like Scott Stamphley *hope* to get when they do things like that. Because Brittany and Mary Kay do not know the rule about ignoring people.

'No,' I said. 'But there's a rule against this.'

Then I burped even louder than he had.

This caused Brittany and Mary Kay to shriek again – and also caused all the people sitting at my table to groan disgustedly, including Scott Stamphley.

That was when Ms Myers came over to see what was going on.

'Excuse me, girls,' Ms Myers said to Brittany and Mary Kay, who were the only ones who weren't at their own table. 'Is there a problem here?'

'Oh, no problem, Ms Myers,' Brittany said, in the sugary-sweet voice she only uses when grown-ups are around. 'We were just telling Allie how much we're going to miss her when she moves away.'

'Well, that's very nice of you,' Ms Myers said. 'But I think you should go back to your seats now.'

'Of course, Ms Myers,' Brittany said.

And the two of them flounced off, squealing things like 'Ew, she's so *disgusting*' and 'I told you! She's practically a *boy*!'

Ms Myers looked down at me as I held my linoleum tile and asked, 'Allie? Are you all right?'

I must have looked as if I was about to start crying or something. I did feel as if I was about to, a little.

'Oh, yes,' I said, trying to smile. 'I'm fine, thanks.'

'Your tile is lovely,' Ms Myers said, about my lino tile. 'Is that Marvin?'

'Yes,' I said. I could feel the tears swimming inside my eyes, fighting to come out. But I was fighting just as hard to hold them back. 'Practically a boy?' How could they say that? They'd seen me do grand jetés. No boy could do that. At least, not in our class.

'Well, keep up the good work,' Ms Myers said, some of her long hair brushing my hand. Then she moved on to see what Scott Stamphley was making (a king snake eating a smaller snake eating a smaller snake, all the while almost being run over by a Corvette, Scott's favourite kind of car).

Over on the other side of the room, I could see Brittany and Mary Kay giggling together. I could also see Courtney Wilcox staring at them all jealously, wishing she was over there giggling with them.

Moving Day

They were probably giggling about my book of rules. Was it really that weird that I kept a book of rules? Rules are important. If it wasn't for rules, no one would know how to act at all.

And then the world would just be full of Brittany Hausers. And who would want *that*?

I wasn't going to give up writing in my book of rules just because Brittany and Mary Kay thought it was weird. I was going to keep on writing in it.

Maybe I just wouldn't tell any more people about it. Like my new best friend, whoever she was going to be. Sometimes it's better just to keep things to yourself.

That's a rule.

Rule #11

When You Finally Figure Out What the
Right Thing to Do *Is*, You Have to Do It,
Even If You Don't Want To

That night after school, Mom and Dad said that Mrs Klinghoffer had called and told them that she'd sold our house for more than the asking price.

So it was over. My war on moving, I mean. I had lost.

They had won.

Our old house doesn't belong to us any more. It belongs to some new people. Some people I've never even met before.

My old room doesn't belong to me any more, either. In fact, I shouldn't be calling it 'my old room'. Technically, it's someone else's new room.

Just like Mary Kay is someone else's new best friend.

To celebrate selling our old house – as if this was something to celebrate – Mom and Dad took us to

Moving Day

Lung Chung, the fanciest restaurant in our town, even though we hardly ever get to go out to eat because when we do we usually misbehave so badly. By 'we' I mean Mark and Kevin. Last time we went to Waffle House, Mark and Kevin permanently jammed the gum-ball machine in the entranceway when Mom and Dad weren't looking by pouring all of the sugar from the packets at our table into the slot where the penny is supposed to go.

And that takes a lot of sugar.

After that, we were asked by the manager of Waffle House never to dine there again.

On the way to Lung Chung, Dad gave Mark and Kevin a talk. The talk went, 'If you do anything at Lung Chung to embarrass your mother we will never take you out to eat again, and you will have to stay home with one of my graduate students while Allie, your mother and I go out.'

You could tell this really scared Mark and Kevin. Because Dad's grad students aren't fun babysitters like Uncle Jay, who stays with us sometimes when Mom and Dad go out. Dad's grad students only know about computers, so they don't know how to do fun things like make microwave brownie soup or slide down the stairs on mattresses. They just know how to write long computer programs, which is what they do while they babysit us. We are supposed to Entertain Ourselves and Not Kill One Another while Dad's grad students work. It's very boring.

Mark and Kevin promised to be good.

I noticed Dad didn't make *me* promise to be good. But that was because he knew Mom was holding the promise of the kitten over my head to make me good. If I wasn't good, I just wouldn't get the kitten.

This was a mistake on Dad's part, if you ask me.

When we got to the restaurant, I checked the plastic pond out front first thing to see if the turtle for turtle soup was still there. It was, sitting on its little island, looking sad and lonely. No one in our town, I was relieved to see, had ordered turtle soup.

But you never know. Maybe someone would order turtle soup tonight. The poor turtle had no idea that this very night might be its last night on earth.

This was possibly the saddest thing I had ever seen.

Uncle Jay met us at the restaurant. When he got to our table he said, 'Congratulations!' to my mom and dad, and hugged them. He gave Mark and Kevin high fives. He tried to give me a high five too, but I told him I wasn't really in the mood.

'What's the matter with Allie?' Uncle Jay wanted to know as he unwound his scarf and sat down.

MOVING DAY

'Allie's not as enthusiastic about the move as some of the rest of us,' Mom said.

'That's the understatement of the year,' I grumbled.

'Why don't you want to move, Allie?' Uncle Jay wanted to know. 'Moving's exciting! You'll be starting a whole new life in a whole new place! You could change your personality – heck, you could even change your name, if you wanted to. Who wouldn't want that?'

'I'm totally happy with my old life,' I pointed out. 'In the old place.'

Which wasn't strictly true, considering what had happened only that afternoon in the art room – you know, with my having lost my best friend and the small matter of the truth about my book of rules having been brutally revealed to the whole of the fourth grade.

But I saw no reason to share this over egg drop soup with Uncle Jay.

'Someone,' Mom went on, 'let Allie watch a certain movie featuring a certain zombie appendage. And ever since then, her interest in living in a certain Victorian house has been on the wane.'

'Oh,' Uncle Jay said.

'Yeah,' Mom said. 'Thanks for that, by the way.'

'Allie,' Uncle Jay said. 'You know that movie about the zombie hand was made up, right?'

'Duh,' I said.

'Allie,' Dad said. 'Don't say duh.'

'Sorry,' I said.

'Well then, what's the problem, Allie?' Uncle Jay wanted to know.

Only I couldn't tell Uncle Jay what the problem was. Because the problem just seemed way too big to get into over dinner.

Besides, by that time the waitress had come over to our table with our sweet-and-sour pork.

Except I couldn't seem to eat mine. I was just too sad. I couldn't stop thinking about how our beautiful house belonged to someone else now.

And I couldn't stop thinking about how Brittany and Mary Kay had made fun of me for keeping a book of rules.

And I couldn't stop thinking about how that turtle had no idea that any minute he – or she – but he looked like a he – could become soup. Every time a new person came into the restaurant, I kept wondering if they were going to be the person to order turtle soup and eat him.

In a way, I felt like I knew what it was like to be

that turtle. Not that anybody was going to eat me. I mean, not yet.

But like the turtle, I didn't have any say over what was happening to me. I mean, that turtle didn't have any choice over whether he got to live in a fake pond in a restaurant, waiting to be eaten, or live in the park across the street where there was a real pond, where other turtles lived.

Just like me. I mean, sure, things weren't working out really great right now at my old school.

But shouldn't I have the *choice* of whether or not I wanted to go to this new school? It wasn't fair that no one was even letting me have a say in the matter.

Just like that turtle.

That was the exact moment that I knew what I had to do. I didn't want to, but, really, what choice did I have? When you finally figure out what the right thing to do is, you have to do it, even if you don't want to.

That's a rule.

I said, 'Excuse me,' interrupting Uncle Jay's story about his new girlfriend, Harmony, who he wanted us all to meet really soon because, besides being his journalism class's star student who frequently got her stories printed up in our local paper's feature section, she was also a really excellent cook and foot massager.

'I have to go to the bathroom,' I said.

'Well, honey,' Mom said, 'you know where it is. You don't have to announce it. Just go.'

I put my napkin beside my plate of mostly untouched sweet-and-sour pork (which is sort of reddish in colour but really it's orangish-pink, so it's OK to eat) and went to the bathroom.

Once I was finished in there and had washed my hands, I opened the door a crack and peeked out. The ladies' room was located directly across from the plastic pond, which was right across from the hostess stand. As I watched, some people came into the restaurant and the hostess, in her shiny Chinese dress, picked up some menus and led them to their table, all smiling and happy.

Now was my chance! No one was looking.

Quick as I could, I darted out of the ladies' room and went to stand by the plastic pond.

I had almost done it! All I had to do was reach down inside, grab the turtle, then run outside and let him go!

Then the Lung Chung turtle would be free!

And so, in a way, would I.

Moving Day

But just as I grabbed the sides of the turtle's slimy, hard shell, I heard footsteps. Someone was coming!

Holding my breath, I lifted up the turtle. He was heavier than I had thought.

Also, stinkier.

That's when I realized he was a snapping turtle. I didn't know they made soup out of *snapping* turtles. I only realized this when the turtle turned his head around and, wondering what was going on, lazily snapped his jaw in my direction.

I couldn't believe it. Here I was trying to save his life, and the Lung Chung turtle tried to bite me! Not like he really meant it – I guess he'd been around the Lung Chung waiters and waitresses so much he was practically tame.

But still. Thanks a lot, turtle.

Trying to keep the turtle as far from my body as I could so his teeth – do turtles even have teeth? If I was going to be a vet, I was going to have to learn these things – couldn't sink into me, I ran for the restaurant's front door.

But too late! Because I heard someone call my name and spun around just in time to see Uncle Jay as he turned the corner on his way to the men's room. When he saw what I had in my hands, he got a very surprised look on his face.

'Allie?' he said. 'What on earth are you doing with the Lung Chung turtle?'

'I'm setting this turtle free,' I said. 'Don't tell anyone!'

'But . . .' Uncle Jay started to say.

And that's when I saw her. The hostess, coming up behind Uncle Jay. She was smiling all nice –

Until she noticed me.

And what I was doing.

Then her smile disappeared. And she yelled, 'Little girl! Where do you think you're going with that turtle?'

That's when I ran through the restaurant's front door for all I was worth.

Rule #12

When You Are Setting a Turtle Free and People Are Chasing You, the Best Thing to Do Is Hide

I knew the hostess lady wouldn't catch me, since she was wearing high heels and a dress. The dress was really tight too.

So I figured she couldn't run very far.

Still, I knew she'd probably go get my dad. And my dad can run far. He plays basketball every Saturday at the Y.

So I knew the best thing to do was hide.

And I knew from playing hide-and-seek with my brothers that the best place to hide is the most obvious – the one place no one would ever think to look. If you were running around downtown with a turtle, where would most people look for you? The park, right?

By the pond. Because that's where you'd most likely take a turtle to set it free.

That's why I didn't go there.

Instead, I decided to wait everybody out in Uncle Jay's car. He never locks it (he says there's nothing in it worth stealing). Also, it was parked right in front of the restaurant. So it was really easy just to dive inside.

I was sitting on the floor with all his CDs, listening to everybody outside yelling about me, when I heard the driver's door open and Uncle Jay slid behind the wheel.

'Allie?' he whispered, like he'd known I was in there all along. Which he probably had. Uncle Jay and I get along pretty well, he says, because we're both independent thinkers.

'Don't tell them I'm here,' I whispered.

Uncle Jay looked down and saw me. The turtle was still snapping in mid-air and kind of making swimming motions with his feet. You could hear him rustling, even though I myself was being excellently silent.

'I won't,' Uncle Jay said, with a kind of smile. 'But you're going to have to come out sometime.'

'I'm not giving them back the turtle,' I said. 'They're just going to make soup out of it.'

'What are you talking about?'

'You know,' I said. 'Like it says on the menu. Just

because no one has ordered turtle soup yet doesn't mean someone won't some day.'

Uncle Jay looked like he was about to laugh. Instead, he said, 'Right. That's totally true.'

'It's not fair,' I said. 'This turtle should have a say in what happens to him. He should be allowed to be free. I'm going to let him go in the park where he can be with his own kind.'

'Well,' Uncle Jay said, 'that's a nice idea. But you know, that turtle has lived in captivity its whole life. I doubt it knows how to look for its own food. And it's starting to get pretty cold out. Soon it will be winter. It might starve. Or freeze to death.'

I hadn't thought about that. Suddenly I realized that my plan of letting the Lung Chung turtle go in the park might not be such a good plan after all.

Actually I hadn't put a whole lot of thought into it. It had been a kind of spur-of-the-moment plan really.

Still.

'But if I give him back,' I said, 'he'll get eaten! I can't stand thinking about him here, knowing at any minute someone could come along, and just . . . order him for dinner.'

Outside the car, I heard my dad yell, 'Jay! What

are you doing? Are you going to help us look for her or what?'

Uncle Jay yelled back, 'Just getting my gloves!' Then, to me, he said, 'OK, Allie. I'll make you a deal.'

'What kind of deal?' I asked. I hate to admit it, but I was crying a little. Mostly because the turtle really did stink and that was making my eyes water.

But also because I knew I was in trouble.

And I hated being in trouble. Which I knew was surprising, considering how much trouble I'd been in lately.

But still.

'I thought we already had a deal,' I said. 'About what really happened to the scuba watch. I never told, you know.'

'This is a different deal,' Uncle Jay said quickly. 'The thing is, I really shouldn't have let you watch that zombie-hand movie. So I kind of owe you one. So the new deal is, I'll keep the turtle. You can leave him here, in the car, and I'll take him home with me tonight to my apartment. We won't tell anyone. It'll be our secret. And in return, you'll stop giving your parents such a hard time about moving into the new house and pretend to be OK with the whole thing. The thing about pretending to be OK with things is that sometimes you actually start to be OK with them. So . . . you never know. Maybe you'll actually start to be OK with the moving thing. What do you think about that?'

I chewed my lip. The turtle living with Uncle Jay was actually an excellent idea. He didn't have any pets, and his apartment was very messy anyway. So it wasn't like he'd even notice the turtle was there.

And I wouldn't have to worry about anyone eating it. So that would be one worry out of many off my mind anyway.

I wasn't so sure about the pretending to like the new house thing though.

'What about the thing that boy said?' I asked.

'What boy?' Uncle Jay asked. Across the street in the park, I could hear my dad calling my name. 'Allie! Allie, where are you? Allie, come here right now. This isn't funny.'

'The boy next door,' I said. 'At the new house. He said the people who used to live there did something bad in the attic.'

'I will use all my investigative powers to determine whether or not this is so,' Uncle Jay said. 'But I'm thinking this guy might have been teasing you. Besides, I'm actually very sensitive to psychic phenomena, and when I was at your new house, I sensed only the most harmonious vibrations.'

I didn't see how Uncle Jay could even say this, considering the dark grey walls and brown floors and all of that.

But I was willing to let that slide since he was being so nice about the turtle.

'Now, what do you say?' he asked. 'Will you come back to dinner?'

The truth was, I didn't really have any other choice. I couldn't sit in Uncle Jay's car holding the Lung Chung turtle for the rest of the night.

So I agreed to his deal.

Uncle Jay got out of the car and went to pretend-look for me in the park with my dad so it wouldn't seem suspicious when I suddenly appeared right after he did. I counted to twenty, and then I put the turtle down on the floor of Uncle Jay's car. It stopped snapping at me and kind of looked around, like, *Where am I? What's going on?*

'You're going to a better place,' I told him. 'One where no one is going to order you for dinner. I promise.' Then I told him I'd come to visit real soon.

Then I got out of the car and went back inside the restaurant.

Everyone was *really* mad at me. Everyone except Mom. She was glad to see me.

At first.

Moving Day

Then she got mad.

'Don't you ever do anything like that again, young lady,' she said when she was done hugging me. 'Do you know how scared I was? Your father and Uncle Jay are still out there looking for you!'

'Yeah,' Mark said. 'And all the restaurant people are really mad at you because you stole their turtle. They said we have to pay for it. And we didn't even get to eat it!'

'Never mind that,' Mom said, giving her credit card to the waitress, who was giving me dirty looks. I wasn't just imagining it either. She was *really* giving me dirty looks. 'Let's just settle our bill. I must say, Allie, I might have expected behaviour like this from one of the boys, but I never expected it from you! What in heaven's name came over you?'

'I just can't stand the idea of someone eating that turtle,' I said.

'Eating that –?' Mom gave me a strange look. 'Oh, *Allie*! No one –'

'See,' Uncle Jay said as he and Dad walked in suddenly. 'She's right here, safe and sound. I told you.'

'Allie.' My dad looked mad. 'There you are. We were looking everywhere. Where's the turtle?'

'Never mind,' Mom said, getting up. 'Come on. We're going.'

'What do you mean, never mind?' Dad asked. 'Allie, just tell us. What did you do with the turtle?'

But I wouldn't tell. Even when the restaurant manager came up and pleaded with me and then told me I was a very bad little girl and that I was going to be in big trouble and that I was lucky they hadn't called the police. That's when Dad stepped in and said, 'Look, we paid for the turtle; cut it out – you're scaring her, OK?'

But the restaurant manager wasn't scaring me at all. I was just thinking how funny it was going to be the next time Dad went over to Uncle Jay's apartment to watch a ball game and he saw the turtle there. Would he even know it was the same turtle?

'Come on,' Mom said after she signed the bill. 'We've had enough celebrating for one night. Let's go home.'

And so we did.

But not before Mark and Kevin made sure they jammed a chopstick into the change-release slot of the payphone right outside the men's room, so no one could ever get change from it again. I high-fived them in the car.

But not so Mom and Dad could see.

Rule #13

You Can't Take Your Rocks with You

I may not be the greatest promise-keeper in the world. I know I didn't do such a great job keeping my promise to Mary Kay on her birthday not to tell anyone I was moving.

But I kept my promise to Uncle Jay.

From the night of my stealing the Lung Chung turtle, I pretended that I was happy that we were moving. I didn't complain any more about the ugly grey walls of our new house. I didn't talk ONCE about how creaky the floors were. I stopped mentioning the zombie hand. I pretended I was happy about moving away from our old house to the new one. I pretended I wanted to start all over in a new school.

And you know what? Uncle Jay turned out to be right. At least, a little bit.

Once you start pretending you feel a certain way, you kind of do start feeling that way. Like, once I started pretending that I was happy to be moving, I kind of didn't feel as bad about it.

I guess it wasn't *that* hard, considering that everybody back at my old school hated me. Well, everybody except Courtney Wilcox.

And since we were moving and packing everything, our old house wasn't that great to live in after all. Everywhere you looked, it was just boxes, boxes, boxes! Who wants to live in a house full of boxes anyway?

Plus, my dad took down my canopy bed and all my shelves to put up again in my new room, which Mom was giving a secret makeover. Since I'd never picked out new wallpaper and carpeting, she'd decided to pick some out for me. She said my room was going to be a surprise.

I pretended to be happy about that too. Uncle Jay, it turned out, was a good advice-giver. It was amazing how my pretending to be happy made Mom happy too.

At least until about a week before moving day. That's when Mom noticed that my rock collection was still sitting in my bedroom, in the ten paper grocery sacks in which I kept it. That's when she

Moving Day

reminded me that I couldn't take my rocks to the new house, and that except for three or four of my best rocks, I had to get rid of them.

'They're not rocks,' I said. 'They're *geodes*. And I'm going to sell them on eBay and buy a cellphone.'

'Whatever they are,' she said, 'you can't take them all to the new house. And there's no time to sell them on eBay and you can't have a cellphone. You have to get rid of them *now*, Allie.'

So that was how I was outside lugging one heavy sack of geodes after another to dump into the big hole in the construction site behind our house when Uncle Jay pulled up into the driveway, and then he and a pretty girl with long black hair got out of his car.

'Hi.' The pretty girl walked over to see what I was doing after Uncle Jay said hi, then went into the house. He'd come over to help my dad take down my brothers' bunk beds. As repayment for this, my parents were going to buy him and Harmony pizza for dinner (I was getting cheesy bread). 'You must be Allie. I'm Harmony.'

'Hi, Harmony,' I said. Harmony looked so clean and pretty, I hoped she wouldn't hold it against me how dirty I was. Returning geodes to the construction site where you found them is a pretty grimy business.

'I was hoping I'd get to talk to you,' Harmony said. 'Jay told me what you did the other night at the Chinese restaurant . . . how you rescued his turtle, Wang Ba. I was wondering if it would be all right if I interviewed you about that for my intensive writing and reporting workshop? I think what you did was amazing and it would make a really good story for my class.'

I shrugged. 'Sure,' I said. 'I guess so.'

'Great,' Harmony said. To my surprise, she took a tiny tape recorder out of her pocket. Then she turned it on and said, 'So, tell me, Allie, in your own words, why you stole that turtle from the Lung Chung Chinese restaurant downtown.'

Telling Harmony the whole story of why I stole the turtle was pretty exhausting. Especially because the whole time I was talking, I still had to keep emptying my bags of rocks over the side of the construction pit.

Then Harmony wanted to know why I was doing that.

So I had to explain about my geodes and how my mom wouldn't let me bring my whole collection to the new house or sell it on eBay. I showed Harmony some of my best geodes, and when she admired how sparkly they were I said she could keep one of them.

Moving Day

But she said unfortunately it wouldn't fit in her handbag.

It was weird, but the whole time Harmony was interviewing me, I couldn't help noticing that Mary Kay Shiner and Brittany Hauser kept walking by my house. I don't know what they were doing. They weren't racing on their bikes, or trying to do pop-ups or anything fun like that (Mary Kay has always been too scared to try a pop-up). They were just walking back and forth. Whenever they passed in front of me they would start whispering and giggling to each other furiously. It was really stupid and kind of annoying. I tried to ignore them, but at one point they started giggling so much that Harmony even looked over at them and went, 'Oh, are those friends of yours? Maybe I should go interview them too. You know, for another perspective to the story.'

'No,' I said quickly. 'Probably you shouldn't. They used to be friends of mine, but now they aren't.'

'Really?' Harmony asked. 'Why not?'

So then I was forced to tell her about the cat in the suitcase incident, and how Mary Kay and Brittany weren't my friends any more. But I asked that those things be off the record. I knew to say that, thanks to a movie Uncle Jay let me watch with him once.

'Oh,' Harmony said. 'I see. You must really love animals to be willing to risk a friendship over a cat like that.'

'Yeah,' I said. I didn't mention the part about how the truth was Brittany was a bat-thrower and Mary Kay just cried all the time, and being friends with them had been no picnic to begin with. 'I guess so.'

After that, all my paper grocery sacks were empty. So I turned around and went inside with Harmony to watch my dad and Uncle Jay take the bunk beds apart. Which turned out to be fun, because they said a lot of swear words when they cut their fingers on the screws, and Mom made them put a quarter each in the swear jar every time.

By the end of the night we had five dollars to put toward a trip to the professional dog groomers' for Marvin.

He's going to look fantastic by the time they're done with him. I hope they put a ribbon in his fringe, even though he's a boy.

Later that night, before bed, I slipped outside to go stand on the edge of the hole and say goodbye to my geodes without anyone else there to see me. Because saying goodbye to some rocks is sort of embarrassing. I could barely see them because the moon was just coming up at that point.

MOVING DAY

I thought about how maybe when the new family who bought our house moved in, their little girl – if they had one – might come outside one day and find my geode collection, and think – like I had – that she'd come across a huge treasure trove of diamonds or something. Maybe she'd think – like I had – that pirates had left them there. Maybe she'd think, 'I'm rich!'

She might be a little disappointed when someone finally broke the news to her that the rocks weren't actually diamonds, just geodes.

But maybe, with luck, she'd turn out to be the kind of girl who could appreciate the beauty of a geode just as much as the beauty of a diamond, even if a geode isn't worth any actual money.

Thinking about that – that maybe my geodes would make some other girl as happy as they'd made me – cheered me up a little. And I wasn't even *pretending* to feel cheered up. Knowing someone else might love my rocks as much as I did made giving them up seem a lot less sad.

So I was able to say goodbye and go back inside with my heart feeling lighter than it had in a long time.

Rule #14

Celebrities Live by a Different Set of Rules from the Rest of Us

A week later it was my last day at my old school, and Ms Myers's fourth-grade class was throwing a good-bye party for me. Well, sort of. Mostly I was throwing it for myself. Mom bought cupcakes – vanilla with chocolate frosting, with sprinkles – at Kroger and brought them over . . . not just for me, but for Mark's class and Kevin's too.

So I had to have a party, whether I felt like it or not. Which, what with the whole Mary Kay still hating me and being Brittany Hauser's new best friend thing, I really didn't. But I didn't have much of a choice.

I should have known things were going to be weird at my goodbye party because things started out being weird much earlier that day. For one thing, when I came out of my house to walk to school that morning, Mary Kay was waiting for me.

162

MOVING DAY

That's right. *Mary Kay* had tried to walk to school with me. Even though I walked very fast ahead of her, I had to listen to her whining, 'Come on, Allie, can't we be friends again?' the whole way. It was so *annoying*.

The thing is, if she hadn't waited until THE DAY BEFORE I was moving away, maybe I would have wanted to be friends again.

But it was a little late NOW.

I thought maybe it had just been because it was my last day and all, and she'd felt bad for being so mean to me, and telling everyone about my book of rules, and all of that.

But then, when I'd gotten to school, Brittany Hauser had started acting all nice to me too, saying my hair looked pretty, and had I done anything different to it (I'd remembered to brush it for once), and asking me if I wanted to sit with her at lunch.

I said no, of course. Why would I want to sit with that big phony?

I got even *more* suspicious when Brittany didn't even get mad when I said no to her sitting-with-her-at-lunch invitation. She just went, 'OK, Allie, whatever you say. Hey, do you want to come over this weekend?'

I went, 'No. I'm moving this weekend.'

I was going to add, 'Besides, I hate you.'

But it's wrong to say you hate people. That's a rule. Even people who are totally hate-worthy, like Brittany Hauser.

'Oh, right,' Brittany said, giggling at her own space-headedness. 'Silly me! I forgot. Well, some other time then.'

'Brittany.' I couldn't help myself. I *had* to find out what was going on. 'Why are you asking me to come over? Don't you remember what happened last time?'

'Oh, you mean about Lady Serena Archibald?' Brittany giggled some more. 'Whatever! I'm so over that. Besides, we had fun, didn't we?'

I hadn't had fun. I didn't even know what she was talking about. Neither did Courtney, when I asked her at lunch.

'Maybe,' she suggested, 'their bodies have been taken over by aliens.'

This seemed the most likely explanation.

I didn't figure out what was REALLY going on until the last period of the day, when it was time for my goodbye party, and Ms Myers called me to the front of the class and put her arm around me, saying in front of everyone how much she was going to miss me.

I was standing up there with Ms Myers, and she was going on about what an asset I'd been to the

MOVING DAY

fourth grade and how well I'd always done in math and science and all.

'And in addition to her many academic accomplishments – Scott Stamphley, if you feel that you are choking on something,' Ms Myers said, because Scott was making gagging noises at all the nice things she was saying about me, 'and would like to be excused, you know where the bathroom pass is – Allie Finkle has also proved herself to be something of an animal-rights activist, bravely saving a turtle from certain death in a cookpot at a popular local eatery . . . at least according to this morning's paper.'

That's when Ms Myers pulled out a copy of the city paper and showed the class – and me, because I hadn't seen it (Mom and Dad had cancelled delivery of our paper due to the fact that we'd be moving in one day) – a big article about my having stolen the Lung Chung turtle and hidden it in 'a safe house' . . . at least according to the article's author, Harmony Culpepper. There was a full-colour photo accompanying the article of me standing next to the construction site behind my house, wearing my cowboy boots and emptying a large bag of geodes into the big hole beneath me. My hair looked very weird because I hadn't brushed it, but you could still totally tell it was me. Under the photo it said, ALLIE FINKLE: JUNIOR ACTIVIST FOR ANIMAL RIGHTS.

That's when I remembered Harmony taking a picture of me with her little digital camera that evening she'd interviewed me for her class. Also, her saying if her professor liked her article he might send it to the local paper for their features section. He only did that, Harmony said, with articles he really, really liked.

Which meant he must have really, really liked her article about me and Wang Ba.

Suddenly I knew why Mary Kay had wanted to walk to school with me again and why Brittany Hauser had wanted to sit by me at lunch.

I was a celebrity.

Seriously. I was famous.

Well, the most famous person in Ms Myers's fourth-grade class anyway.

'Allie, we're going to miss you so much –' Ms Myers went on.

'Not all of us,' Scott Stamphley said. Only you couldn't really tell that's what he'd said, because he'd said it in the form of a cough. Only, I happen to know how to speak cough because I practically invented that language.

I gave Scott a dirty look.

Moving Day

'I beg your pardon, Scott,' Ms Myers said. 'If you need to be excused for a drink of water, you know where the pass is.'

'I'm all right, Ms Myers,' Scott said.

'Good,' she said. 'Well, I just wanted to add that even though I know Allie is going to love her new school, we're going to miss her very, very much, and that's why we made her this . . . right, class? To remember us by.'

'Right,' said various people in my class, including Brittany Hauser, who said it the loudest. Which also made it the most phony, incidentally.

That's when Ms Myers brought out a large piece of poster roll on which everyone in the class had written a message to me saying how much they would miss me – or not, as in the case of Scott Stamphley, who'd written only, *Smell ya later, Stinkle!*

'Wow,' I said. I noticed that Brittany and Mary Kay had only signed their names, which showed that the class had made this before I'd become a celebrity and before they'd decided they wanted to be friends with me again. 'Thanks, everybody. This means so much to me.'

Because it's a rule that even if someone gives you something that you don't really want, you should still say thank you.

'And now let's have some of these delicious cup-cakes your mom brought,' Ms Myers said.

'Delicious chemical cakes, you mean,' I heard Scott Stamphley whisper. The boys sitting around him laughed.

'Sure,' I said to Ms Myers, pretending I hadn't heard Scott. 'Let me pass them out, Ms Myers.'

'Thank you, Allie,' Ms Myers said. 'But are you sure you don't want any help?'

'Oh, I'll help!' Brittany Hauser nearly broke her arm she flung it in the air so fast volunteering to help. 'Let me, Ms Myers. Let me!'

'That's OK,' I said, with a smile that I hoped was as sugary-sweet as the cupcakes. 'I'm happy to do it myself.'

'OK, Allie,' Ms Myers said. 'If you're sure . . .' She handed me the big white pastry box from Kroger.

'Oh,' I said, 'I'm sure.'

I went slowly around the room, handing out the cupcakes. When I got to Mary Kay, she went, in a soft voice, tears glistening in her eyes, 'Listen, Allie. What you did for that turtle . . . that was so . . . so brave.'

'Thanks, Mary Kay,' I said. 'But I didn't do anything you wouldn't have done.'

I knew this was a total lie. No way would Mary

Moving Day

Kay have saved Wang Ba. She never would have had the guts.

'Listen,' Mary Kay whispered, 'I know we've been fighting a lot lately. And I'm really sorry I told Brittany about your book of rules. I shouldn't have done that. I'm really sorry. I want you to know you'll always be one of my best friends, Allie. Always.'

I thought that was very interesting, considering that up until yesterday Mary Kay hadn't thought of me as a friend at all. Then, suddenly, I'm a celebrity animal activist and she thinks of me as her best friend again?

'Gee, thanks, Mary Kay,' I said, as fake as she was being. Because two can play that game.

'Don't mention it,' Mary Kay said, taking a big bite of her cupcake.

When I got to Courtney Wilcox, she said, 'Here, Allie, this is for you,' and handed me a little box. I had to put down the cupcakes in order to open the box, which turned out to have half a silver heart necklace in it.

'See?' Courtney asked excitedly, showing me what was around her neck, which was the other half of the silver heart necklace. 'By each of us wearing half of the broken heart, it shows we're friends even if we're not together. My mom got it at the mall. I thought you'd like it.'

I did like it. What I liked about it was that Court-ney's mom had to have gotten it for her before she knew I was a celebrity animal activist. Because I only became one this morning.

Courtney Wilcox, unlike Mary Kay, was being completely unfake.

'Neat,' I said. I put the necklace on, then held out the box from Kroger. 'Have a cupcake.'

'Thanks,' Courtney said, and took a cupcake.

Then I turned to Brittany. I had saved her for last.

'Cupcake?' I said to her.

'My, these look delicious,' Brittany said, reaching for the last one.

'Here, allow me,' I said.

I picked Brittany's cupcake up and pretended like I was going to hand it to her.

But instead, I smashed it in her face. Then I ground it in, for good measure.

'Food fight!' Scott Stamphley yelled.

And the next thing I knew, everyone who had any cupcake left in Ms Myers's fourth-grade class was throwing whatever was still in their hands. By some sort of unspoken agreement, the girls were throwing theirs at Scott Stamphley, and the boys were throw-ing theirs at Brittany Hauser and Mary Kay Shiner . . . I think mostly because Brittany was the one who started screaming 'Not in my hair' the loudest when bits of cupcake began flying (also, of course, because she didn't have any cupcake to throw back). And Mary Kay, of course, was the one who started crying. This made them both irresistible targets.

At least to me.

So, really, my last five minutes at Walnut Knolls Elementary were the best five minutes of school ever.

Even if I did end up in the principal's office.

The other thing was, I had to sit by Scott Stamphley while we both waited for our parents to come pick us up.

And he kept singing a song about diarrhoea that, by the way, I have known since second grade.

Finally, I couldn't take it any more.

'I've known that song since kindergarten,' I told him, which was an exaggeration, but only a slight one.

'Yeah?' Scott stopped singing. 'Well, why don't you sing along then?'

'Because it's stupid,' I said.

'Like your face?' Scott asked.

I couldn't believe I was stuck in the principal's office on my last day of school. With Scott Stamphley. I knew nothing bad was going to happen to me, since Mrs Grant, our principal, is always very understanding . . . unlike my new principal, Mrs Jenkins, seemed like she'd be.

Still.

'Like everything about you,' I said. 'Only to infinity.' I really meant it too.

'Yeah,' Scott said. 'Well, you really nailed Mary Kay Shiner with that last bit of frosting.'

I couldn't help smiling at this unexpected compliment. I actually couldn't believe he'd noticed.

'I did,' I said, 'didn't I?'

'She screamed,' Scott said, 'just like a girl. Did you see when I got Brittany Hauser in the head with all those leftover sprinkles from inside the box?'

'She's going to be finding sprinkles in her hair for weeks,' I said with relish.

'*Ooooh, my hair*,' Scott squealed, in a dead-on imitation of Brittany.

'Hey, that's good,' I said. 'You should be in the talent show at the end of the year.'

'Come on,' Scott said modestly.

'No,' I said. 'Really. Nothing would make her madder.'

'You think?'

'I bet she'd even cry.'

'You know, Allie Finkle,' Scott Stamphley said, 'you're all right, sometimes.'

Moving Day

This was such an astonishing remark to have come from a boy like Scott that for a moment I was stunned speechless. What had just happened? Had Scott Stamphley actually said something nice to me?

Before I could say anything in reply, however, my mother showed up, looking mad. Right behind her was Scott's mom, not looking too happy either.

'Allie Finkle,' Mom was saying. 'What is this I hear about you? What is that in your hair, young lady? Is that . . . is that CUPCAKE? The cupcakes I BOUGHT for you? You had a FOOD FIGHT? Are you nine years old, or FIVE? Ms Myers couldn't be more disappointed in you . . . Oh, that is it. THAT IS IT. When I get you home – If you think you're getting a kitten now –'

I have to admit, hearing that Ms Myers was disappointed in me, not to mention the part about my not getting a kitten any more, made my eyes fill up with tears. I probably would have started crying too, if I hadn't remembered Scott Stamphley was right there, watching me. Plus how totally great it had felt, rubbing that frosting into Mary Kay's hair.

I looked over at Scott. His mom was saying a lot of the same things to him that mine had said to me, only not the part about the kitten, obviously. And she didn't call him 'young lady'.

I noticed he wasn't crying, though, either. In fact, he was calmly picking bits of cupcake off his shirt. And eating them.

This, I realized as my mom dragged me off to our car, was going to be my last image of Walnut Knolls Elementary: Scott Stamphley eating bits of my good-bye cupcakes off his shirt.

Goodbye, Ms Myers. Sorry I disappointed you.

Goodbye, fourth-grade class. I forgot my poster with all your messages on it.

Goodbye, Brittany Hauser. I guess I don't really hate you. But I don't really like you very much either.

Goodbye, Courtney Wilcox. I'm sorry we didn't get to be best friends for very long. I really like the necklace your mom got me at the mall.

Goodbye, lunch lady. Thanks for all the chocolate milk, even though I didn't pay for it.

Goodbye, Buck the horse. I hope you liked the Fruit Roll-Ups.

Goodbye, Mary Kay. You were never a very good best friend because you cried too much and never let me be the girl lion so I always had rug burns. Still, I really am sorry I stuck that spatula down your throat.

Goodbye, Scott Stamphley.

Goodbye forever.

Smell ya later.

Rule #15

Don't Judge a House by How It Looks Before You Fix It Up

I was still pretending I was excited about moving – even though I totally wasn't, especially now that I for sure wasn't even getting a kitten – when Mom and Dad took us over to the new house to show us the big surprise.

The big surprise was our rooms. Mom had taken time off from work and secretly been working on them while we were at school, and they were finally ready. Mom wanted us to see how great they were before we moved in, also so she could make any changes in case we didn't like them.

Not that it mattered, since we were still going to have to move in whether we liked our rooms or not.

So I pretended in the car to be happy about going to see our new house.

But inside, I wasn't so happy. Inside, I was

thinking about running away. Because it was all so unfair. I mean, I had never wanted to move in the first place, or change schools, or throw out my rock collection. And now the one thing – well, besides the fact that I was going to get to go to school with Erica and Sophie and Caroline and maybe have Mrs Hunter as my teacher – that I had been looking forward to – Mewsette – was being taken away from me.

That was just wrong. So wrong.

It seemed like it would totally serve Mom and Dad right if I ran away. Especially considering the fact that I was a celebrity animal activist now – which had turned out to be a pretty big surprise to my parents, but still hadn't kept them from taking away my kitten – and all. If I just took my overnight bag – because all the rest of my clothes were packed up into boxes, I just had a few things, like my toothbrush and a change of clothes and my Anno Doll (which is the Raggedy Ann doll that I sleep with, which I've had since I was three and that's all dirty and had a leg broken off where Marvin chewed it when he was a puppy, but Mom sewed it back on), and my book of rules stuffed into an overnight bag – and left, I could probably make it to Uncle Jay's apartment building. It's a long way to campus from our old house but from the new house it's only a few blocks, actually.

Moving Day

And then I could just live there with Uncle Jay and Wang Ba and get a kitten and no one could tell me not to. Uncle Jay would never tell me not to. He'd never even notice a tiny kitten, his apartment is so messy.

But I never got around to running away, because I guess I fell asleep instead of packing, and by the time I woke up we had to get ready to go see the new house.

Still. I was thinking about it. Don't think I wasn't.

I knew I wasn't going to like my room no matter what Mom had done to it. How could I? You can't make a dark, drafty room warm and bright, no matter how much paint you throw at it.

But I had promised Uncle Jay to pretend.

So I pretended to be excited all the way over in the car. I pretended to be excited all the way up the front steps to the house. I pretended to be excited as Mom was unlocking the door.

And then I walked through the door.

I have to admit . . . I was surprised by what Mom had done to the place in just a few short weeks. While I'd been busy at school being tortured by Brittany Hauser and Mary Kay, Mom – with Dad's help – had been busy painting, dusting off the chandeliers, changing the lightbulbs in them and scraping the floors, making them all shiny and nice-looking.

Oh, she hadn't gotten to *everything* yet. The back passageways were still dark and scary-looking. And the backyard was still just mostly dirt patches with some scraggly grass growing in it here and there. And the new stove and refrigerator and dishwasher hadn't arrived yet, so there were just empty spaces in the kitchen where these things would go.

But all the spiders were gone.

Until we got upstairs to the third floor where the kids' bedrooms were, and I saw that all the spiders were in Mark's room. Only, fortunately, they weren't alive. They were on his wallpaper.

And not babyish cartoons of spiders either, but actual grown-up drawings of them, and insects too, with their scientific Latin names written next to them.

Of course, Mark freaked out, he was so excited. Don't ask me why anyone would want to live in a room with drawings of spiders and beetles and bees and flies and wasps and ants all over his walls. My brother wanted to, apparently.

And Kevin was only slightly less happy than Mark with his room. He had pirate wallpaper – pictures of pirate ships and skull-and-crossbones flags. But it wasn't velvet wallpaper. Because there really is no such thing as velvet pirate wallpaper . . . at least that Mom could find.

She gave him blue velvet curtains though. So he was happy about that anyway.

I didn't expect much when I pushed on the door to my room. I was preparing a happy smile to plaster on to my face anyway. I figured once all my stuff was moved into it I'd grow to like my room. Eventually. In, like, twelve years.

I never thought I'd see what I saw when I got the door all the way open.

And that was a room that was even prettier than my room back in the old house.

I don't know how Mom and Dad had done it, but they had. With a combination of cream-coloured wallpaper with tiny blue flowers on it and a matching blue carpet – not to mention white lace curtains and the window seat Mom had promised Dad would make me – they had made what I thought was the worst room in the whole house into the nicest room I had ever seen.

I just stood there in the doorway staring at it, smelling the new paint smell, hardly able to believe my eyes, while Kevin and Mark stood behind me, going, 'Whoa, that's fancy,' and 'See, Allie? I told you.'

Mom went, 'Well, Allie? What do you think?' sounding very proud of herself.

I was in such shock, I didn't even remember to pretend-smile. I said, '*I love it!*'

Because I did.

'Oh, I'm so glad,' Mom said. 'And what do you think of the window seat Daddy made you?'

'Well,' Dad said, 'Home Depot made it, really.'

'I love it too,' I said, running over to it and bouncing on the cushion. Sitting on it, I could look out down to the street below. The leaves on the trees were changing, and all I could see beneath me was a kaleidoscope of colours, orange and yellow and red and brown, like a quilt spread out beneath me. It was like I could jump out the window and bounce on it, a trampoline of colours. It was the prettiest thing I had ever seen. Almost as pretty as my room. I could sit in that window seat and look out for hours. Who even cared if I couldn't see the electrical tower from my room any more?

'Good,' Mom said. 'We're glad you feel that way. But we're not through showing you things yet. Come over here.'

I got off the window seat and went back out into the hallway.

MOVING DAY

That's when Dad pulled on the cord to the attic door in the ceiling.

'Dad!' I yelled. 'Don't do it!'

But it was too late. Dad was pulling down the folding ladder to the attic. The springs attached to it were making pinging noises.

'Come on, Allie,' he said. 'I'm going to show you there's nothing to be afraid of. We're all going up here.'

'Sweet,' Mark said, and started climbing the ladder after Dad.

'Oh, no, you don't,' I said, grabbing the back of Mark's trousers. 'Dad, what are you trying to do, get us all killed?'

Dad's head and shoulders had already disappeared into the attic. 'It's perfectly all right, Allie,' he called down. 'There's nothing up here except a few boxes of junk. Look, come up and I'll show you.'

'Let go of me, Allie,' Mark said, trying to kick my hand away. 'I want to go up with Dad.'

'Mark,' I said. 'Stop it! I'm trying to protect you!'

'Allie,' Mom said, 'let him go. You should go up there too. It's the only way to prove to yourself that there's nothing up there to be afraid of.'

I let go of Mark. I had to, because he'd been about to kick me in the face. He scrambled up the ladder.

I sighed. I knew Mom was right. But . . . what about the zombie hand?

'Whoa!' I heard Mark yelling from the attic. 'Come up here, you guys. You have to see this. It's incredible!'

I looked at Kevin.

'*I'm* not going up there,' he said. 'I don't want to get dusty.'

'Go on, Allie,' Mom said. 'I've been up there. I'll stay here with Kevin.'

Sighing again, I put my foot on the ladder. And I started climbing. I could see my dad's head at the top of the ladder against the rafters of the roof of the house. Also, I could see some sunbeams shining in from somewhere. The attic didn't, I have to admit, look that scary.

And when I got to the top of the ladder and looked around, I saw that it wasn't scary at all (except for the being-on-top-of-a-ladder part). It was just a long room, with a really low, slopey roof. And it was practically empty, except for a few boxes. And my dad and Mark were bending over those, opening them up and tipping them over to reveal that all that was inside them was . . .

'Christmas cards!' Mark said in disgust.

I didn't believe him at first. But then I went to look

and saw that it was really true. Each of the boxes was full of Christmas cards. Dozens and dozens and dozens of them. Maybe hundreds.

Used ones. They were written in. Some of them even had pictures. And they were really old. Like, twenty years old!

'Well,' Dad said, 'it's no zombie hand, I'll admit. But this one is pretty scary.' And he held up a Christmas card that was a family photo of some ugly people with really stupid-looking hair on vacation at Disney World.

'Pick up those boxes and take them down to the dumpster while we still have it,' Mom yelled up the ladder.

'Come on,' Dad said. 'Hand me down a box, each of you.'

So that's how we cleaned out the attic to get it ready to put our own junk in. I was throwing a box of the Ellises' old Christmas cards in the dumpster in our driveway when I heard a voice call my name and turned around to see Erica in her front yard, waving to me.

'Hi, Allie!' she called, smiling. 'Are you moving in today?'

'Not today,' I said, running over to meet her at the hedge across the alley that separated our two yards.

I saw that Missy was out in the Harringtons' front yard too, practising her baton twirling, and that Erica's older brother, John, was there as well, raking leaves. 'We'll be moving in tomorrow.'

'Oh, good,' Erica said, smiling even more. 'I can't wait! Sophie and Caroline told me to say hi. We were all so happy when Mrs Hunter said you'd be joining our class!'

'Wait,' I said. 'She *did*? I *am*?'

'You didn't know that?' Erica started jumping up and down. She was also yelling, like she always seemed to when she got excited about something.

'NO,' I yelled back, jumping up and down too. 'I bet my parents were going to tell me later as part of the surprise!'

'What surprise?' Erica wanted to know.

'The surprise about my room,' I said. 'Do you want to see it? They fixed it up really nice!'

'Sure,' Erica said. 'Just let me run inside and tell my mom where I'm going so we don't have the same disaster we did last time.'

Erica turned around and ran inside her house. I watched Missy throw her baton high in the air, then do a spin and catch it just before it hit the earth. John, meanwhile, leaned on his rake and went, 'So, Allie. How's it going?'

Moving Day

'Good,' I said, a little bit suspiciously. That's because I was wondering if he was going to bring up the thing about the attic.

Sure enough, he did.

'So,' he said. 'Heard anything strange coming from . . . you know where?' And he pointed behind me, to the peak of the roof of my house.

'If you mean, have I heard any weird noises from the attic,' I said loudly, 'no, I have not. Because there's nothing in there but some old boxes of Christmas cards. Which aren't even there any more, because we just cleaned them out.'

'Well, that's all you can see in the daytime,' John began. 'But at night, when everyone else has gone to sleep, I've heard some pretty strange things coming from that attic. Like someone was trying to get out –'

'Stop teasing me,' I said to him in my meanest voice. 'I'm nine years old, you know, not a baby. I know there's no such thing as ghosts, not to mention zombie hands. You should be ashamed of yourself, a boy your age, trying to scare little girls. What do you think your mother would say if she knew what you were doing?'

John blinked a few times. Then he said, 'You're not going to tell her, are you?'

'I don't know,' I said, folding my arms across my chest. 'Maybe I will.'

At that exact moment Erica came bursting out of the house and ran over to where I was standing.

'My mom said it was all right,' she announced, leaping over the hedge. 'Let's go!'

'Good,' I said. 'Come on!'

We started to run to my front door but then, at the last minute, I remembered something and said, 'Hold on a minute, Erica. I forgot something.'

And I ran back to the hedge and said, 'John.'

John looked up from his raking. 'What?' he asked.

I burped as loud as I could.

'That's what,' I said.

Then I ran back to grab Erica's hand and pull her inside.

Rule #16

Don't Be a Braggart

The moving truck showed up really early the next day. So early that Mom and Dad weren't even out of bed yet, and there was enough swearing that we got five more dollars for Marvin's trip to the groomers'.

So I woke up to the sound of the moving men honking their horn and Mom and Dad swearing. I jumped out of bed and got dressed real fast. Because I knew there was a lot to do.

Mark was very impressed by the moving truck, which he said was an eighteen-wheeler. Kevin pointed out that the moving men wore special belts. Dad said this was to keep them from getting hernias when they lifted heavy things. We asked what a hernia is, and Dad said it's when your stomach explodes. Kevin said he'd like to see that, and I agreed.

So we sat on the steps for a while, hoping to see one of the moving men's stomachs explode. That's when Mom got the idea to send all us kids to spend the rest of the day with Uncle Jay at his apartment, where we'd be Out of the Way.

'No junk food for lunch, please,' Mom instructed Uncle Jay when he arrived to pick us up, giving him a twenty-dollar bill. 'Something semi-healthy, like pizza and breadsticks.'

'Sure,' Uncle Jay said, slipping the twenty in his pocket. 'I hear you.'

As soon as we got to Uncle Jay's, he went, 'Who's up for Hot Pockets?'

We were all up for Hot Pockets, of course. We always like staying at Uncle Jay's, because he lets us have a whole can of Coke – each – instead of making us share one in glasses. Also, he has a television that is almost as big as my bed. He doesn't have much else in his apartment, except for a futon couch. But the TV more than makes up for it. When we watch cartoons on it, it's like we're actually there under the sea *with* SpongeBob.

The first thing I did when I got to Uncle Jay's was check on Wang Ba. The turtle was living in the bath-tub in Uncle Jay's room-mate's bathroom (only Uncle Jay doesn't have a room-mate any more because he says room-mates stifle his creativity). Uncle Jay had made it all nice in the bathtub for Wang Ba, with rocks for him to climb on and some plants and plenty of water to swim around in. It was like Wang Ba's own private pond.

It's hard to tell if a turtle is happy or not. But I have to say, Wang Ba looked pretty happy. I mean, for a turtle. He didn't smell as bad as he had before, for one thing.

'Why so glum, chum?' Uncle Jay wanted to know, leaning in the doorway with my ham and cheese Hot Pocket on a plate for me in one hand and a full can of Coke in the other.

'Oh,' I said. I guess I'd looked sad. 'I got in trouble at school on Friday for starting a cupcake fight.'

'Awesome,' Uncle Jay said.

'Not awesome,' I said, taking my Hot Pocket and Coke. 'Now Mom says I can't have a kitten.'

'Obviously, your parents are unaware of your unique status in the community as an animal-rights activist,' Uncle Jay said. 'Anyway, Allie, I'm sure if you cool it for a few days and try to help around the house and stuff, your mom'll come around. She always does.'

'I don't know,' I said. 'She was pretty mad.'

'Well,' Uncle Jay said, 'I realize he's no kitten. But you'll always have Wang Ba.'

I looked down at the Lung Chung turtle. And I remembered how the other night I'd planned on running away to come live with Uncle Jay. Being here in the daytime made me realize I was kind of glad I hadn't. I love Uncle Jay and stuff. But his Hot Pockets were kind of cold in the middle.

After four hours of the Cartoon Network and about three more of video games, Mom and Dad finally called to say the movers were gone and Uncle Jay could bring us to the new house. So we got into the car and he drove us over.

It was dark by the time we pulled into the driveway. But for the first time ever, there were lights on in the windows of the new house.

And I have to admit, it didn't look nearly as scary as it usually did.

In fact, it looked kind of . . . well, homey.

And, OK, Mom and Dad hadn't had time to put curtains up anywhere but in our rooms or anything.

And inside, hardly any of the boxes had been unpacked, and almost none of the furniture was where it was really supposed to go because the movers had kind of just dropped it all off and left.

But with our stuff inside, the new house looked like . . . well, it looked like home.

And upstairs, in my new room, Dad had put up

MOVING DAY

my canopy bed, and my shelves were on the walls, and my clothes were in my closet, and my books were where they were supposed to be.

And with the lamp shining on my bedside table and my lace curtains blocking out the dark, it still looked like the nicest room in the whole world.

And after I'd hidden my book of rules where it belonged (under the slats beneath the bed), I realized it really *was* the nicest room in the whole world.

And, OK, the bathroom across the hall still needed some work – the tiles on the floor were super cold, and the water that came out of the sink was brown at first from no one having used it in so long.

And, yeah, the attic door still looked creepy up there, with that cord hanging down from it.

But the new house, I was starting to realize, wasn't so bad. Especially when, as I was getting ready for bed, I heard Mark and Kevin going, through the heating grate between their two rooms, 'Houston, this is the space shuttle. Are you there, Houston? Over.'

'Houston, this is the space shuttle. We read you. Over.'

'Well, honey,' Mom said, coming into my room to check on me as I was getting under the covers. 'Is everything OK?'

'Everything's OK, Mom,' I said. And I didn't just mean the room. Even though she did.

'Really?' she wanted to know. 'You can tell me if something's wrong, you know, Allie. It won't hurt my feelings.'

'Nothing's wrong,' I said. And I kind of was surprised to find that Uncle Jay was right. I wasn't pretending any more. Everything really was fine. I mean, there'd be school to get through next week – my first week as the new girl, in a new class, with all new people to get to know.

But I'd deal with that later. Right now, everything was good.

Well, almost everything.

'Well, that's good to know,' Mom said, tucking me in. 'I meant to tell you something, but in all the excitement of moving day, I forgot. I got a call today from Brittany Hauser's mother.'

Uh-oh. Had the chemicals in the Kroger cupcake I mashed in Brittany's face caused some kind of permanent damage?

'Don't worry,' Mom said. 'It wasn't about the cupcake fight. It was about Lady Serena Archibald.'

Oh, no! I don't know why, but I thought this could only be bad news. I chewed my bottom lip. Something bad had happened. Something bad to do with my letting Lady Serena out.

'What happened?' I asked, dreading Mom's answer.

'Well,' Mom said. She seemed to be having trouble holding back a smile. 'It seems that when you let Lady Serena Archibald out' – *I knew it!* – 'she met a gentleman cat. And now she's going to have kittens.'

I gasped. Wait . . . this was *good* news! 'She *is*?'

'Yes. And since they don't know who the father cat is, the chances are extremely unlikely that they're going to be pure-bred Persian kittens. So Mrs Hauser will be giving away Lady Serena Archibald's kittens for free. And she wanted me to make sure that I let *you* know that you are going to have first pick of the litter when they're born in a few weeks.'

I was so excited I jumped up from under the covers. Then I remembered what Mom had said on Friday, in the principal's office.

'But wait,' I said. 'You told me I can't have a kitten any more.'

'Well,' Mom said, 'your father and I talked it over. And because you've been so good about moving – *for the most part* – we changed our minds. You can have a kitten after all.'

I screamed so loud, Mom had to put her hands

over her ears. 'You mean I get to have one of Lady Serena Archibald's kittens?'

'Not if you don't stop screaming like that,' Mom said, lowering her hands. 'But yes, I guess you do. First pick.'

I threw my arms around Mom's neck and gave her a big hug. I was so happy I was almost crying. I couldn't believe it. I was going to get a kitten after all! And not just any kitten, but a kitten from the most beautiful mom cat of all time, Lady Serena Archibald!

Mewsette was going to be the best cat ever.

'OK,' Mom said, laughing, as I kept on hugging her. 'Go to sleep now. If you can. We have a lot of unpacking to do tomorrow.'

I snuggled down under the covers.

'I can't wait to tell Erica,' I said sleepily. 'I'm going to run over first thing in the morning.'

'After breakfast,' Mom said.

'OK,' I said. 'But right after that . . .'

'But don't tell her in a braggy way,' Mom said. 'Because no one likes a braggart.'

'What's a braggart?' I asked.

'Someone who brags a lot,' Mom said.

'Like Brittany Hauser? She's always going on about how, for her tenth birthday, her mom is going to rent a limo and take all the girls in the class to the Build-a-Bear store, and every girl is going to get to build her own bear, then go to Pizza Hut to have individual pizzas, then take the limo home.'

Brittany had also pointed out I wouldn't be invited to do any of this.

'Exactly like that,' Mom said. 'That is a good example of a braggart. Don't be like that.' She flicked off my bedside lamp. 'Now, go to sleep, Allie.'

But as soon as I heard the steps stop creaking – which meant that Mom was all the way downstairs and was another good thing about this new house, I was discovering . . . you always knew when a parent was coming up or going down the stairs – I turned my bedside lamp on again and got out my notebook from under the bed.

Then I wrote down *Nobody likes a braggart* in my book of rules.

It was my first rule for the new house.

I had a feeling I was going to learn a lot of good rules in this house.

Then I closed my book, hid it beneath the bed, got back under the covers, turned out my light and closed my eyes.

Because Mom was right. I had a *lot* to do tomorrow.

Allie Finkle's Rules

- Don't stick a spatula down your best friend's throat.
- Everything that goes up must come down.
- Don't let go of helium balloons outside.
- Treat your friends the way you'd want them to treat you.
- Never eat anything red.
- Always wear a helmet when you're skateboarding because if a car hits you your brain will splat open, and kids like me will spend their time waiting for the cars to go by so they can cross the street looking for bits of your brain the ambulance might have left behind in the bushes.
- Don't get a pet that poops in your hand.
- Don't scare your little brothers.
- If you don't want a secret spread around, don't tell it to Scott Stamphley.
- You should only say nice things to your friends, even if they're not true.

Moving Day

- Brothers – and parents – can be very insensitive.
- You're not supposed to hate people, especially grown-up people.
- It doesn't count if it doesn't hurt.
- You can't let your family move into a haunted house.
- If someone is yelling with excitement, the polite thing to do is yell back.
- Whatever Brittany Hauser says, just do it if you know what's good for you.
- Never be catcher when Brittany Hauser is up to bat.
- Liquorice is gross.
- First impressions are very important.
- You can never make a second first impression.
- It's not polite to correct a grown-up.
- Don't put your cat in a suitcase.
- Listen politely when a grown-up is telling you something, even if you already know it.
- You can't let your guests starve.
- When you do something wrong, always apologize (even if it's not entirely your fault) – you can always explain later.
- If you get a new best friend, it's rude to show off about it.
- Say thank you when someone gives you a

compliment even if you aren't sure whether it is a compliment.

- Pretend like you don't care when someone is insulting you, and don't cry. That way, you win.
- Sometimes (but not always) it's better just to keep things to yourself.
- When you finally figure out what the right thing to do *is*, you have to do it, even if you don't want to.
- When you are setting a turtle free and people are chasing you, the best thing to do is hide.
- You can't take your rocks with you.
- Celebrities live by a different set of rules from the rest of us.
- Even if someone gives you something that you don't really want, you should still say thank you – if it is something they meant kindly.
- Don't judge a house by how it looks before you fix it up.
- Don't be a braggart.

So what happens next to Allie?

Find out in . . .

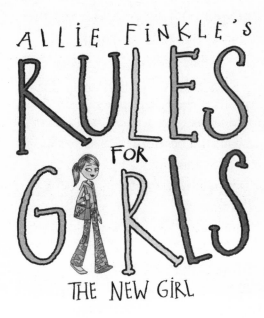

ALLIE FINKLE'S
RULES
FOR
GIRLS
THE NEW GIRL

Out now!
Read the first chapter over the page

Rule #1

Mom didn't think I should wear a skirt with jeans on my first day at my new school.

'Allie,' she kept saying, 'you can wear a skirt *or* jeans. But not both at the same time.'

This argument was not helping the nervous butterflies that were fluttering around in my stomach, considering the fact I was less than one hour away from starting my first day at Pine Heights Elementary, my brand-new school.

I tried to explain about how my new plaid skirt flared out when I twirled around. Which was totally great, and a very important trick to be able to do, especially on your first day at a new school.

2

THE NEW GIRL

Except what was going to happen if I climbed the jungle gym and hung upside down at recess?

I'm not saying I was *going* to do this. I'm just saying it *could* happen, and if it did and all I was wearing was a skirt, the boys in the playground would totally see my underwear.

This was not something you would particularly want to happen on your first day at a brand-new school.

I don't see how Mom couldn't tell that this was a problem.

Fortunately it was a problem that was easily solved. It was solved by wearing jeans under my skirt.

'Allie,' Mom said, 'why don't you wear tights under your skirt? Or leggings?'

Which was a nice idea. But, as I reminded her, all my tights and leggings were still packed – along with all my pyjamas – since we had just moved to our new house two days before. And we couldn't find the box they were packed in. We could only find the box with my jeans, shirts and skirts in it.

My tights, leggings and pyjamas were not the only things we'd packed and couldn't find. We also couldn't find the hairdryer, the cereal bowls and most of the pots and pans.

But this was OK, because our new stove hadn't come yet, so we had nothing to cook on anyway.

Personally I didn't see why wearing my plaid skirt with jeans was such a bad thing. I thought my skirt looked really, really good with jeans. So good that I decided to wear it on my first official day at Pine Heights Elementary.

Because *When you are starting your first day ever at a brand-new school, you have to wear something good, so people will think you're nice.* This is a rule.

First impressions are important. Everyone knows this.

It's true that I had already been to Pine Heights Elementary School once before and met my new teacher (Mrs Hunter) and some of my new class-mates (Caroline and Sophie, and of course Erica).

But while I'd already been over to Erica's house multiple times, and she'd been over to mine, because we lived next door to each other, I hadn't really gotten to know Caroline and Sophie yet (other than playing a game they'd made up called queens with them at recess the day I'd met them).

And there were still lots of people I hadn't met at all yet, and I wanted to make sure I got off on the right foot with them.

Getting off on the right foot with people is

important. If you don't get off on the right foot with people, it could ruin your whole year.

Which was why I knew wearing a skirt with jeans would be just the right thing to do.

It was just too bad Mom didn't think so.

Fortunately Mom had bigger things to worry about. Like that my little brother Kevin wanted to wear his pirate costume to his first day of kindergarten at Pine Heights Elementary. Really, in comparison, my wearing a skirt with jeans was nothing.

'But Halloween was last month, Kevin,' Mom kept saying.

'I don't care,' Kevin said. 'It's important to make a good first impression. Allie said so. Allie said it was a rule.'

Mom was too busy chasing Kevin around, trying to get him out of his pirate costume, to notice I was still wearing my skirt with my jeans. So I sneaked into the kitchen to see what was for breakfast. What was for breakfast was popcorn.

'I can't find the cereal bowls,' Dad explained.

'We could just eat it out of the box,' my brother Mark said, stuffing popcorn into his mouth. Mark is in the second grade. Mark did not have butterflies in his stomach about his first day at a brand-new school. Mark never has butterflies about anything, such as, for instance, jumping off the roof of his friend Sean's house, which he did once, thus breaking his arm. This is because Mark doesn't think about anything except bugs. And sports. And possibly trucks.

'Once, at Sean's house,' Mark said, 'we poured milk right into the cereal box and ate out of it with spoons.'

'That's disgusting,' I said.

'No it wasn't,' Mark said.

'I'm sure the milk leaked,' I said. 'Out of the box and all over the place.'

'No, it didn't,' Mark said. 'Because of the seal-tight plastic bag inside.'

'Well, I'm not doing that,' I said. 'I'm not sharing a box of cereal with you. I don't want your germs.'

'We have the same germs,' Mark said. 'Because we're related.'

'Actually, we don't,' I said. 'Because I don't pick my nose and eat it like some people I could mention.'

'The thing is,' Dad said while Mark was denying that he picks his nose and eats it, 'no one is sharing a box of cereal. Because I can't find the spoons either.'

'What's going on in here?' Mom said, running into the kitchen. She was holding Kevin's pirate hat, but she didn't have the rest of Kevin. That's because he'd disappeared into one of the many secret passageways of our new house, which is more than a hundred years old. 'Why does it smell like popcorn?'

'That's what we're having for breakfast,' Mark said.

'No,' Mom said. 'How did this happen? Whose idea was this?'

Mark and I both pointed at Dad. He said, 'I don't see what the problem is. Popcorn is made of corn. People eat cornflakes for breakfast all the time.'

'Popcorn has no nutritional value,' Mom said.

'Yes it does,' I said. 'Popcorn is high in fibre. Fibre is good for you.' I know this because I did a report on fibre for science once. Corn, which is something they grow a lot of in my home state, is full of fibre. *You need a lot of fibre in your diet to help digest your food.* This is a rule.

'But they haven't had any dairy,' Mom protested.

'I put butter on it,' Dad said. 'And they've got orange juice.'

Mark and I raised our measuring cups of orange juice to show her. We were drinking out of measuring cups because Dad couldn't find the drinking cups.

Mom looked at the ceiling. 'Please don't tell your new teachers you had popcorn for breakfast today,' she said before racing out of the kitchen after Kevin, who was hiding until the last possible minute so Mom would have no choice but to let him wear his pirate costume to school.

I knew the feeling.

'My new teacher, Mr Manx, would think it was cool if I told him I had popcorn for breakfast,' Mark said. 'Probably.'

'Well,' Dad said, 'Mom would appreciate it if you didn't tell him anyway. When you come home for lunch, things will be more organized. I promise.'

That was when the doorbell rang. The doorbell on our new house isn't a normal doorbell where you push a button and it goes *ding-dong*. That's because our house is so old, the doorbell is a crank that you turn, and it rings a bell attached to the other side of the wall that goes *brrrring*, like a bicycle bell.

But if you cup your hand over the bell part while someone is turning the crank, it just goes *brrurp*. We found this out after playing around with the doorbell so many times that Mom finally said, '*No child whose last name is Finkle may touch the doorbell or they will not be allowed to watch television for two weeks.*' This is a rule. Not one of mine, one of the family rules.

'That's Erica!' I yelled because I was so excited. Erica had said she'd stop by to walk to school with me on my first day.

I raced to the front door and flung it open. Erica was standing there in her hat and coat, looking as excited as I was.

'Hi, Allie!' she yelled.

'Hi, Erica!' I yelled back.

'I can't believe it's your first day at Pine Heights!' Erica yelled.

'I can't believe it either!' I yelled back.

Then we both jumped up and down for a while until Mark came and said, 'Girls,' disgustedly, then brushed past us and ran outside to join some boys he saw riding by on their bikes.

'Wait!' Mom screamed from deep inside the house.

'Why does your house smell like popcorn?' Erica wanted to know.

'Because we had it for breakfast,' I said, getting my hat and coat. 'We packed the cereal bowls and can't find them. I can't find my tights or leggings either. That's why I'm wearing jeans with this skirt.' I twirled to show Erica my skirt.

'Wow, that skirt is so cute,' she said. 'It's like my sister's skirt for baton twirling.'

This made me really happy to hear, because Erica's older sister, Melissa, who goes to the middle school and is an expert baton twirler, is really, really cool, even though she mostly doesn't speak to us and stomps away with her nose in the air whenever we're around.

'Here we are,' Mom said, showing up with Kevin just as Erica and I were about to walk out the door.

Erica and I looked at Kevin. He was still wearing black pants, black boots and a white shirt with long puffy sleeves. Mom had gotten him to give up his red sash, skull-and-crossbones hat, eyepatch and sword.

'At least she could have let me keep my eyepatch,' Kevin said, looking sad.

'You look really good,' Erica assured him.

'Why don't you just put on normal clothes?' I asked him. It's a pain having such a weird brother. Between him and Mark, I sometimes wonder how I got so cursed in the big-sister department.

'*You're* wearing jeans with a skirt,' Kevin pointed out.

'I don't want boys to see my underwear in case I hang upside down from the jungle gym,' I explained.

'Well, I want everyone to know I'm a pirate,' Kevin said.

'They will,' Erica assured him.

'OK,' Mom said in a very fake-cheerful voice as she appeared with her coat and purse. 'Are we ready to walk to school together?'

I could see now that Mark had been smart to run

ahead with those boys. *There is nothing wrong with walking to school with your mom and dad on your first day. Except everything.* Which is a rule, by the way.

Or it will be when I write it in my special notebook for writing rules in that I keep in my room.

'We can walk by ourselves,' I said quickly.

'What about Kevin?' Mom asked.

'Oh, we'll be happy to walk Kevin, Mrs Finkle,' Erica said, taking Kevin's hand.

I didn't know about that. I mean, no one asked me. I wasn't happy to walk Kevin to school.

But it was better than having my *parents* walk to school with us.

'Sure,' I said, taking Kevin's other hand. 'We'll walk Kevin.'

'OK,' Dad said. He had on his own coat. 'You girls walk Kevin. And we'll walk behind you and pretend we don't know you. How's that?'

This wasn't exactly what I had in mind. But it was better than nothing.

'OK,' I muttered.

Erica and I steered Kevin through the door. Outside, the leaves, which had already started changing colours, were beginning to fall from the trees and blanket the sidewalk. It was also cold.

'How come you don't want to walk to school with

your parents?' Erica wanted to know. 'I think they're funny.'

'They're not so funny,' I assured her, 'once you get to know them.'

'Having popcorn for breakfast is funny,' Erica said. 'My dad would never do that. And letting your brother wear a pirate costume for his first day of school is funny. Even wearing a skirt with jeans is kind of funny – although it looks really good.'

I thought about what Erica said. I didn't think it was true. The Finkles weren't funny. The truth was, Finkles were actually exceptionally talented. Especially my Uncle Jay, who Erica hadn't even met yet, because he lived in his own apartment on campus, who was probably the most talented Finkle of all. He could bend one of his toes so far back it touched the top of his foot. Plus, he had double-jointed thumbs.

I wished I had special skills like that. If I did, I wouldn't have any trouble at all making friends at my brand-new school, or have to wear a special skirt that twirled in order to get people to like me. *If you have special skills or talents, such as having double-jointed thumbs, other people will automatically like you right away.* That's a rule.

It's true that Erica liked me. But she hadn't asked me to be best friends or anything. Probably a skirt that twirled wasn't going to influence her decision one way or another. But I had to do what I could.

When we were halfway to the school and had reached the stop sign at the first (completely non-busy) street we had to cross to get to Pine Heights, I noticed there were two girls walking towards us from the other direction. Erica said, 'Oh look! It's Caroline and Sophie.'

And it was.

'Oh my gosh, it's your first day,' Sophie yelled, jumping up and down when she saw me. 'This is so exciting!'

'I know,' I yelled back. Because *When someone is yelling at you with excitement, it's polite to yell back.* This is a rule. 'I'm so nervous! I have butterflies!'

'Don't be nervous,' Caroline said. She was the first one to stop jumping. I was starting to realize this because Caroline is actually quite serious. 'Just be yourself. Is this your little brother? Why is he dressed that way?'

'Because I'm a pirate,' Kevin informed her.

Caroline looked from Kevin to me.

'He's in kindergarten,' I explained with a shrug.

'Are those your *parents*?' Sophie whispered, noticing my parents hanging around behind us. They waved, and Sophie and Caroline waved back politely.

'Just ignore them,' I said, pulling on Kevin to get us moving along again.

'They wanted to walk Allie and Kevin to school today,' Erica explained. 'But Allie wouldn't let them, so now they're just following us.'

'Aw,' Sophie said, 'that's so cute!'

'Allie's dad made them popcorn for breakfast,' Erica said. I could tell she was enjoying herself, talking about how funny the Finkles were. This was turning out to be one of her favourite subjects. 'Because he couldn't find any cereal bowls!'

'You're not supposed to tell anyone about the popcorn,' I said to her. 'Or, at least, not any teachers.'

'That's OK,' Caroline said. 'One time we ran out of sandwich meat, so my dad just made us mustard sandwiches. They weren't very good. My parents are divorced,' she explained 'and my big sister and I live with my dad. It can be hard sometimes.'

'It must be,' I said sympathetically.

'My dad's a really good cook,' Sophie said. 'Last night for dinner he made us spaghetti Bolognese. My dad does all the cooking in our family, because my mom is working on her dissertation. And besides, she's a terrible cook. She burned potpourri once.'

'You can't burn potpourri,' Caroline said.

'Yes you can,' Sophie said. 'If you go to the mall

and leave it simmering on the stove, the water in it evaporates and then the potpourri smoulders, and then the smoke-detector goes off and the neighbours call the fire department. It was so embarrassing.'

I appreciated what Caroline and Sophie were trying to do – make the butterflies in my stomach go away.

And it was kind of working. Almost all the butterflies in my stomach had disappeared.

Before I knew it, even though we hadn't been walking particularly fast, our feet were tromping on the dead leaves that lined Pine Heights Elementary's playground. I could hear the shrieks of encouragement as kids (including my brother Mark) played kickball while waiting for the first bell to ring. I could see people on the swings pumping their legs to go higher and higher. I saw clusters of other kids just standing around, doing nothing but looking at other kids looking at them (which included me).

That's when the butterflies in my stomach came right back. In fact, they turned from butterflies into great big swooping bats banging around inside me. Because I couldn't help thinking, what if none of those kids in the playground liked me? What if the only people who talked to me all day were Erica, Caroline and Sophie? Which would be OK . . . but I didn't want them to get sick of me, not on my first day. Then I'd have a whole year of no one liking me but those three. That would be terrible! I mean, for them.

It was right then that something truly awful happened.

Kevin let go of my hand and also Erica's and ran towards the jungle gym – I guess because he saw some kids his own age playing on it.

To me Kevin just looked normal. I mean, the fact is, he wears his pirate costume all the time, such as to the grocery store, to story hour at the library, and to Dairy Queen for his favourite cone, vanilla twist butterscotch dip, which he is always careful not to spill on his red sash.

But I heard some of the kids standing in a cluster nearby – they were girls, big girls, too, maybe fifth-grade girls – start to laugh. When I looked over at them, I saw that they were laughing . . . at Kevin! That had to be what they were laughing at, because they were looking right at him.

They were laughing at my brother.

And then they looked over at me. Then they started whispering to one another. Which meant they could only be whispering about me. But why? What was

I doing wrong? *I* wasn't wearing pirate trousers and boots beneath my down parka.

Then I remembered: I was wearing a skirt with jeans. I'd insisted on wearing a skirt with jeans, in spite of the fact that my mom had tried to talk me out of it.

Oh, this was terrible!

And that's when it hit me. Maybe what Erica had said was really true – the Finkles *were* funny. Maybe the Finkles were *too* funny . . . too funny to fit into someplace new. Like a new school . . . a new neighbourhood . . . a new anywhere.

Oh, why had I let my parents talk me into moving? Why had I let them convince me to start at a new school, where I didn't really know anyone and where people might think Finkles were funny?

And why – why, oh why – had I worn a skirt with jeans on my very first day at my brand-new school?

A selected list of titles available from Macmillan Children's Books

The prices shown below are correct at the time of going to press. However, Macmillan Publishers reserves the right to show new retail prices on covers, which may differ from those previously advertised.

Meg Cabot

Allie Finkle's Rules for Girls: The New Girl	978-0-330-45376-9	£5.99
Allie Finkle's Rules for Girls: Best Friends and Drama Queens	978-0-330-45381-3	£5.99
Allie Finkle's Rules for Girls: Stage Fright	978-0-330-45378-3	£5.99
Allie Finkle's Rules for Girls: Glitter Girls	978-0-330-45379-0	£5.99
Allie Finkle's Rules for Girls: Blast from the Past	978-0-330-45380-6	£5.99

For older readers

The Princess Diaries	978-0-330-48205-9	£5.99
The Princess Diaries: Take Two	978-0-330-48206-6	£5.99
The Princess Diaries: Third Time Lucky	978-0-330-48207-3	£5.99
The Princess Diaries: Mia Goes Fourth	978-0-330-41544-6	£5.99

All Pan Macmillan titles can be ordered from our website, www.panmacmillan.com, or from your local bookshop and are also available by post from:

Bookpost, PO Box 29, Douglas, Isle of Man IM99 1BQ
Credit cards accepted. For details:
Telephone: 01624 677237
Fax: 01624 670923
Email: bookshop@enterprise.net
www.bookpost.co.uk

Free postage and packing in the United Kingdom